A CHRISTMAS AT JEKYLL ISLAND CLUB

ROMANCE AT THE GILDED AGE RESORTS
BOOK FIVE

BLOSSOM TURNER

Copyright © 2023 Blossom Turner

All rights reserved. No portion of this book may be reproduced or transmitted in any form or by any means - photocopied, shared electronically, scanned, stored in a retrieval system, or other - without the express permission of the publisher. Exceptions will be made for brief quotations used in critical reviews or articles promoting this work.

The characters and events in this fictional work are the product of the author's imagination. Any resemblance to actual people, living or dead, is coincidental.

Unless otherwise indicated, all Scripture quotations are taken from the Holy Bible, Kings James Version.

ISBN-13:

Listen, O daughter, Consider and incline your ear: Forget your own people also, and your father's house.

Psalm 45:10, NKJV

As this novella is the beginning of a new series, I think of both my grandmothers, Bertha Dorn and Olga Kuerbis, who bravely left their war-torn countries in Europe and sailed to a world unknown. Talk about new beginnings. How brave these women were as they stepped off that ship onto Canadian soil. How inspiring to me now as I take on this late-in-life career of writing. Their strength in the Lord is a beacon that shines on in my heart and encourages me to give my best to God as they both did.

CHAPTER 1

December 1906
Jekyll Island Club, Georgia

Savannah Marie Ensworth threw back her head and laughed. "Who me? Go to church? I dare say not." She carefully pulled her long white traveling gloves from each finger and threw them on the bed. "I thought by the time I got here, you'd have come up with something interesting to do on this boring island. Church is certainly far down my list of exciting."

"Just hear me out." Elizabeth almost bounced with enthusiasm. Her carefully pinned auburn hair had sprigs of curls bent on escaping the confinement. "I know you're bored. What a dreadfully dreary life. Your daddy's money. Your mama's good looks. Your insatiable need for adventure—"

"You know I don't look anything like my mother,

and you're one to talk, Elizabeth. You live just as privileged a life."

"I know. But there's a difference between you and me."

"Do tell." Savannah glided to her bedroom window with her back straight and her head held high. She gazed out from the third floor of the clubhouse. A peek of the Jekyll River sparkled between the ancient live oaks draped in Spanish moss. Stirred by a sharp breeze, the surface waters tossed about, as restless and agitated as the inner workings of her troubled soul. She blew out an exasperated puff of air. There was nothing new under the sun, and coming back to this mind-numbing island for the winter season year after year might stimulate her parents, but it did nothing for her.

"I'm quite content with the status quo," Elizabeth said. "I'll marry Walter, have a few kids, and forever feel blessed at what I've been born into. Visiting this glorious private island with its fishing, hunting, tennis, golf, and endless beaches will never be a hardship. You, on the other hand, are never satisfied."

Savannah turned from the window. "Ouch, that would hurt if you weren't my best friend and I didn't know you better."

Elizabeth laughed as she dropped, unladylike, onto Savannah's bed. "You know I love you."

"Hard to tell sometimes."

"Come to church with me tomorrow and you'll see how much."

"Come on, Elizabeth. Church is your thing, not mine. Dreary old men talking about hellfire and brimstone is not to my liking."

"That's just it. He's most definitely not a dreary old man."

"Who?"

"Reverend Joseph Bennett. He's young. Handsome as they come." Elizabeth giggled. "Intelligent, witty, and he's single." Her eyebrows danced. "And every eligible young lady on the island has suddenly become a church attender."

Savannah rolled her eyes. "So?" What did she care about the reverend's looks? She had her pick of men, and not a one could pique her interest. How could a preacher possibly change that?

"So...come and check him out for yourself. You can't be the only woman who doesn't know what all the fuss is about."

"He'll be gone in two weeks. Not worth my Sunday morning beauty sleep."

"Because the season is just getting started, he'll be here the entire month of December rather than the changeover of clergy that usually happens every two weeks. My Walter knows him from the mainland and has nothing but good things to say about the man. I met him myself last Sunday, and well...he's different, and interesting, and all I could think about was how much you'd probably like him. Could make your December stimulating."

"Why, that's preposterous."

What was Elizabeth thinking? Savannah didn't like most men. The young were immature and self-centered. The older ones thought their women had to fall into line. Savannah had no intention of ever needing a man, much less becoming a submissive wife. She was the sole heiress to her daddy's banking fortune. And with her brains and gumption, she had little use for a husband who would stifle that freedom.

Things would be easier if she was plain and didn't appeal to the numerous suitors who had already proposed marriage and been disappointed. Savannah caught a glimpse of herself in the three-paneled mirror on her dressing table and turned to the side. Her thick blond tresses were piled and pinned to perfection with a section that cascaded down her back. A finely sculptured face with high cheekbones and startling dark eyes, not to mention the expensive tailored traveling suit made to accent the positive, gave evidence of why she indeed attracted bees to the honeypot.

Elizabeth jumped up from the bed. "I've got an idea. No better yet...a dare. I know how much you enjoy a challenge."

Avoiding her friend's gaze, Savannah glanced around the spacious bedroom where a few embers still flickered in the ornate stone fireplace. She refused to take the bait.

"Come to church with me tomorrow and see if your interest is not piqued. And if it is..."

Savannah had to admit, she was a tad intrigued. "Then what?"

"Then you shall agree to my challenge."

"Which is?"

"You work your magic and see if you can get a man of the cloth to fall under your spell. Because as much as you go on about never marrying to be under a man's thumb, this reverend tells my Walter much the same. Women are nonsensical and unsuitable to aid in his calling. He has yet to meet one that would be worth the distraction. Seems you both are most agreeable on the dispensableness of the opposite sex. Could be a match made in heaven."

"Highly unlikely, but I do rather enjoy the conquest."

"I know you do."

Savannah had yet to meet an eligible bachelor who was not either intent on getting close to her daddy's money or enthralled with her comely looks. Most of the time, it was both. There would be no contest. "All men are the same, Elizabeth. And if I so desire, I could have the reverend eating out of my hand by Christmas." She laughed. The sound came out brittle and harsh. "But first, let me see if he arouses even an inkling of interest on my part."

"Yes. Let's." Elizabeth clapped her hands together.

The winter season of 1906 had barely begun on Jekyll Island, yet the polished pews of Faith Chapel were unduly brimming with activity from the female gender. Savannah slipped into a pew halfway down the aisle, not too close and not too far from the pulpit. Elizabeth and Walter squeezed in beside her.

"Good morning, Sunshine." Elizabeth squeezed Savannah's arm.

Savannah rolled her eyes at her friend. That little nickname was a direct hit at the fact she was not a morning person and didn't have a ray of sunshine to spare before a cup of coffee and a leisurely breakfast.

"Have you had your coffee?" Elizabeth giggled.

Savannah lifted her chin and looked away. She would not bless that comment with a reply.

The morning sunlight filtered in through a stained-glass window, highlighting Mother Mary with the Christ child. The three wise men bowed in subservience, offering gold, frankincense, and myrrh. Savannah looked away. There was something in their faces that rankled, a humbleness she could not understand. Why would they have traveled for many moons, these richly adorned, kingly men, only to bow to a mere child? Did that really happen? She doubted it very much.

She focused on the architecture. With a love for structures, her mind took in every detail. The classic A-frame Gothic design, tidewater red-shingle construction on both inside and out, solid beams, and detailed, handcrafted, carved work around the front interior arches above the altar and windows. A luxurious carpet lay beneath her feet. Simple but classic. No expense was spared. That was the way of their exclusive millionaire's club—nothing but the best.

Upon entry, she had not failed to notice the beautiful setting of palmettos, live oaks with Spanish moss draping in silvery strands, and breathe in the sweet smell of hyacinths blooming in a flower bed along the walkway.

Her attention to detail was both a curse and a blessing. Like that preposterous hat Myrtle Pearson was wearing. Who was she trying to impress? The black velveteen cloche with pleated ivory silk lining and ridiculous ostrich plume looked completely overdone in the heat of their near-tropical paradise and the modesty of a church service.

"There he is." Elizabeth's nails dug into Savannah's arm even through the light gloves she wore. Her other hand raised and waved. One would think Elizabeth was enamored with the man herself.

Savannah smiled at Elizabeth, taking her time to turn her head discreetly toward the front. She was not prepared for the instant attraction that assaulted her senses. Her pulse quickened, much to her chagrin. Her eyes collided with the reverend's, and she fell into a pool of mysterious, dark beauty. She wrenched her gaze away, feigning great interest in the stained glass behind him.

But that one look, like a deep breath, soaked in his strong face, wide forehead, well-defined chin, and six-foot-plus frame with wide shoulders that slimmed to a trim waist. The much ado was certainly *not* about nothing. It grated her that she had fallen as captive to his perfection as all the other women now in rapt attention to the soft cadence of his rich baritone voice.

Her gaze furtively darted from reverend Joseph Bennett to her trembling hands that wrung together in her lap, and back again. She was quite used to dapper men dressed in their finest, but this one was different. His plain black suit looked like something out of the Victorian era, with the clerical collar the only distinction to his line of work. Yet the man spoke with a confidence that did not match the pauper he must be.

And to think he was brave enough to speak out against the excesses of the rich, in a congregation of the wealthiest people in the nation. What was this about the social responsibility of each believer to attend to the broken-hearted, the lonely widow, the homeless children living on the city streets, the hungry, the poor? Even to the outrage of suggesting the outcasts be invited into one's home, all according to Isaiah 58? Now that was a religion she had not heard preached before. She shifted in her seat. Half of her wanted to get up and run out of the building, and the other half wanted to run to the front and fall on her knees, begging God for that kind of purpose in her seemingly pointless existence.

The last hymn was sung, and Savannah turned for the door. It took every bit of her breeding and training in etiquette to not break into an all-out run. The decision was made. She would stay as far from that man as she could. He was too dangerous in every way.

CHAPTER 2

"Savannah, wait up." Elizabeth's singsong voice carried the plea on the wind.

Savannah ignored her. This island was not big enough for the distance she needed to put between herself, Faith Chapel, and that preacher. She lifted the folds of her skirt, creasing the fine cotton without care. Walking faster was all that mattered. She required time to sort the confusion, and a conversation with Elizabeth would not help.

At the bend in the road, where Elizabeth could no longer see her, Savannah ducked down an oyster-shell path toward the river. She would forgo lunch and sit by the water and think. Nature had a way of soothing her tattered soul, but it also increased a need for something unnamed.

They ate too often, anyway. With breakfast, lunch,

afternoon tea, and a formal dinner, there was a revolving door of non-stop delicacies. The imagery that the preacher had so masterfully woven of starving urchins on the streets of New York, the ones she skillfully avoided, made her shiver in the warmth of the midday sun. That sermon was exactly why she hated church. She always felt guilty and selfish, as though she was supposed to be doing something. Was God really so demanding?

She plopped unceremoniously down on a bench beneath an ancient, gnarled live oak. The calm waters of the Jekyll River flowed lazily by. A flash of yellow caught her eye. The warble of a Yellowthroat stopped her breath. So pure. So beautiful. Tears filled her eyes. Why was she so emotional as of late?

Minutes passed into an hour. Savannah pulled her white gloves from sweaty palms and lifted her tendrils of thick hair to allow the cooling breeze from the river access to the back of her neck.

She had no desire to attend the afternoon tea at the Hollybourne Cottage. Mother would be most annoyed that she didn't show, and she would endure a tongue lashing, to be sure, but she couldn't bring herself to move. A despondency she had never felt before edged in.

There had to be more to life than the tedium of afternoon teas, over-indulgent dinners, shopping, and socializing. Even on the island with its array of pleasures different from those offered in New York, a void filled her soul. A longing. For something she could not define.

Savannah closed her eyes. The quiet waters meandering beneath the thick foliage, lapping upon the muddy shore, accompanied by the sound of songbird, calmed her ragged soul. So different from the clamor of the city... Maybe this was why she hated the island—too quiet with too much time to think. And she was not at peace with her thoughts.

"Hmm, I see someone's been sitting in my chair. And she even looks like Goldilocks too."

Savannah jumped. Her eyes flew open wide.

The reverend stood tall and imposing before her. A grin hitched up both sides of his handsome mouth. He held out his hand. "Joseph...Joseph Bennett."

That was forward of him. She liked to see herself as progressive in her thinking, but she quite preferred tradition in this circumstance. Her removed gloves made the situation more intimate. Didn't he know that a man of lesser status, and a stranger at that, did not initiate a handshake? Yet she met him halfway to ease the awkwardness. "Savannah...Ensworth."

His strong fingers encircled hers. A tremor shivered up her arm at his touch. His mysterious dark eyes danced with shadows of gun-metal gray and black. He leaned closer and spoke with genuineness. "Happy to make your acquaintance. Your name suits."

Now what did he mean by that? Did this man know nothing about etiquette? In truth, she shouldn't even be allowing this unchaperoned moment. Mother would have a bird at the forwardness.

He gently slid his hand from hers and dropped his arm to his side.

A strange sense of loss tugged at her insides.

"Savannah..." He rolled the name slowly over his tongue. "It has a regal sound."

"And Joseph...one you would expect of a preacher."

"I can see by your reaction that I may have been too familiar. Please excuse me if I have offended you. I don't usually run in these circles."

Savannah smiled to ease his discomfort. Of course, he didn't. His mere attire gave that away.

"Are you the daughter of Henry and Anna Ensworth?"

"One and the same. You've met my parents?"

"I rarely forget names and faces. They were on the Jekyll Island Steamer that picked us up in Brunswick last week, but I don't recall seeing you."

"I held off coming as long as I could and arrived yesterday with my Aunt Mary. I don't care for all this tranquility." Her hand flung out toward the river. "I much prefer the hum of New York City."

"And yet here you sit near the water's edge rather than dining in luxury."

"And you. Why are you not partaking?"

"I can't handle too much rich food. May I?" He pointed to the bench beside her.

He really didn't know the rules, but she was most

curious, rarely having the privilege of association with the more common folk. She nodded. "Seems you think this bench is yours, anyway. Are you about to scare poor Goldilocks away?"

He slid to the bench beside her and turned her way. "I would never scare one as beautiful as you."

Oh, there it was again. That instant attraction most men communicated at first blush. Would there ever be a man immune to the outward shell? One that desired to get to know her for who she was, not what she looked like, or the money her daddy had?

"Please don't get me wrong," Joseph said. "That statement is a matter of fact. God created you with little room for improvement, but I've always been far more fascinated by what's inside a person's heart than what I can see on the outside."

Was he reading her mind? "Really?" She tried to keep the sarcasm from her voice.

"Yes, really. I believe if women or men tried half as hard to improve the inner person as they do the outward, this world would be a far better place."

"I'm sure that's easy for you to say, looking the way you do." Had she said that out loud?

"So you like what you see?"

Her cheeks burned hot. "I could ask the same, but it would be most unladylike."

He laughed. The crinkles around his eyes danced. "Your honesty is most becoming."

His propensity for directness unnerved her. His

sermon had made her uncomfortable, but this conversation even more so. She grabbed her gloves and stood with a ramrod straightness. "I must be going."

"Without answering the question?"

She lifted her chin. "I'm sure you're quite aware of your attractiveness, Reverend Bennett. You do not need another admirer."

"It is not admiration I desire, Miss Ensworth, but an authentic relationship. Not sure how that is obtained without getting the obvious out of the way." He stood to full height which towered over her.

"The obvious?"

"Yes, the obvious. From the moment our eyes met this morning there was an instant attraction."

"Why, I never..." Savannah huffed and began walking.

"Am I wrong? Or have you never had someone be so forthright? Or you've never felt an instant attraction before. Or you've never—"

Savannah stopped and whirled around almost slamming into his wide chest. She looked up. "I've never met anyone as insufferable as you."

He had the nerve to laugh out loud. A clear, booming laughter that echoed across the river and back again. Dimples on both sides of his mouth framed a beautiful smile.

"And I've never been attracted to a socialite before. I know that it can never work, as we're worlds apart, but I thought to get the awkward out of the way so we can be friends."

"You would like to be my friend?"

"I have a whole month, and I'd love to learn how the wealthy think, their etiquette in which I most assuredly fall short, and what their views are on how the rest of the world lives while they bask in luxury."

"Meaning?" Was he intentionally rude, or merely naïve?

"Take for instance the opulence of the clubhouse compared to the servants' quarters. I honestly don't understand...but don't want to judge erroneously. I know that seeing things through another person's eyes is the best way to learn."

"You're serious?"

"Absolutely. And you could ask me questions about how the common person thinks, lives, struggles."

"Why would you think I care?" She started walking up the path towards the clubhouse, and he fell in step beside her.

"I noticed the compassion in your eyes when I began to speak about the unfortunates living on the streets of New York."

"You could see the expression in my eyes by mere glances halfway up the aisle of church?" Her voice held a tinge of sarcasm. Why did he have to read her so accurately?

"Am I wrong?"

She hesitated. "No."

"Then we'll be a perfect pairing. With no possibility for what can never be, we can embark upon an unfettered friendship. It'll be so refreshing to not have that constant tension I find with most women who want more than I'm willing to give. Pressure you most likely endure as well."

What can never be...his words sounded as though she was some sort of plague he needed to avoid. Well, maybe, just maybe, she'd take Elizabeth up on her little challenge. It would be quite delightful to stoke the ember of attraction into a flame and have the confident Reverend Bennett not so sure of himself.

Savannah stopped on the path just short of the tree canopy giving way to the open view of the clubhouse. "I understand, Mr. Bennett. Things do get most complicated when affections are not returned. I'd be delighted to strike up a friendship."

"That's wonderful."

"But the first obstacle we'll have to overcome is how we're going to do this when in your world, friendship is easily navigated, but in mine, it is not. Even to have this unchaperoned conversation is strictly forbidden."

"You're best friends with Elizabeth and her fiancé, Walter Nielsen, correct?"

"Yes."

"The four of us could do things together. Could we not?"

"Brilliant idea." She smiled up at him. "But for today, it's best if I return to the clubhouse alone."

He touched the tip of his bowler hat. "I understand. I'll head back down to the river and finish a much-needed walk."

Savannah nodded. "Until next time." She gave him the demure smile she reserved only for those with whom she wished to keep the mystery going and turned away.

Her step had an extra spring. She had something to look forward to. It would be quite entertaining to embark on a so-called friendship with the good reverend and watch him succumb to her charm.

The imposing circular tower turret of the clubhouse poked above the trees. The broad veranda wrapped around three sides of the four-story brick structure. Balconies and balustrades with whimsical arches invited one in.

In comparison to the dull row of the servant's annex, the opulence of the clubhouse with its cypress-shingled roof and vivid Victorian colors stood tall and grand. But in contrast to Savannah's home in New York, it paled in comparison. Maybe that was why she had never paid attention to the haves and the have nots.

And now, thanks to Joseph Bennett, she had a particular reason to notice.

CHAPTER 3

Why had he gone and done that? Joseph pulled his bowler hat from his head and ran a hand through his thick hair. It had been so entertaining to shock the blond heiress from her slumber and be brazen enough to admit he was attracted to her. He smiled at the thought of her feeling the same. He was right about that.

But wasn't he supposed to flee temptation, not procure a way to be in its presence throughout his stay on the island? Wouldn't you know it, the first woman who actually made his heart slam into his chest was as ill-fit to be a preacher's wife as a lioness was to a cage.

He brushed a smudge of dust from his felt hat, and with a sweep of his hand, swung it back on top of his head. He best walk farther and pray harder, for something about this woman hinted his whole world was about to change.

The crunch of the oyster-shell path beneath his boots created a cadence to his prayers. *God, I've waited so long to feel something. Anything. Why her? Clearly, she's not the one. And yet...as our eyes met this morning...*

How his heart had sped up. And then to feel the disappointment as she ran out before he could make her acquaintance, only to find her sitting all alone.

He'd headed out for this walk to clear his head of her intoxicating lure, but then there she was, dressed in a soft yellow that matched the gold of her beautiful hair. His reaction to the touch of her hand, free of those ridiculous gloves women of gentry must wear even in this stifling heat, was telling. And her blush, how adorable. Despite clearly being flabbergasted by his honesty, she'd spoken with an inbred control and moved with an elegance uncommon to his walk of life, reminding Joseph where he came from.

Why had he suggested such an impossibility...a month of friendship? His gut twisted into a knot.

She needs Me. The response dropped into his spirit just as clearly as if God had spoken aloud.

He threw his hands up.

Great. This was all God's doing. This island, when his father had been the one supposed to come before he reworked his schedule so that Joseph could, as Father said, "step up in the world." And then Elizabeth with her teasing way, insisting she had a friend she wanted Joseph to meet. One look at Savannah and immediate attraction had washed over his stony heart, creating feelings he didn't know what to do with. And then a walk along the river, only to find that which he was trying to outrun. What were the chances that they would both skip lunch and arrive at the same spot?

God, with You, I know there are no chance happenings. If Savannah needs You, who am I to balk at the circumstances? But Lord, what about what I need?

~

"Where have you been?"

Savannah turned toward the suite door her mother burst through. No big surprise. She had prepared herself for the tongue lashing.

The tall, slim woman glided across the room. Always the image of perfection, from her Paris ensemble to the swath of silver hair swept back from her forehead against the remaining black in a flawless coiffure, she exuded elegance.

"How utterly embarrassing to show up to the Maurice's for afternoon tea without you in hand. I told you their son, Albert, had asked about you the other day and I had assured him you were arriving yesterday and would be present today."

"Mother." Savannah rose from the windowside chair where she had been lounging. "When are you going to realize I'm a grown woman? Aren't you the one always spouting that at twenty-two, I'm almost an old maid? Surely, I deserve the right to make my own schedule."

The feathers in her mother's hat fluttered in a breeze created by the fitful shake of her head. "Don't you dare get haughty with me. As long as you live in our household, you will respectfully abide by our wishes."

"And missing an afternoon tea is somehow disrespectful?" Savannah stifled the puff of air building in her lungs.

"My duty as your mother is to see you suitably married. And so far, you've turned down every eligible pairing your father and I have suggested. Not to mention the ones that came knocking."

"What does a boring afternoon tea with a garden full of women have to do with marriage?"

Mother closed the few feet between them, her sculpted features pale and pinched. "You are an unusually bright young lady. Don't pretend you don't understand. If Albert Maurice is asking about you, he is clearly interested. And one does not snub Charlotte Maurice or her family."

Savannah stepped back to give herself space from her mother's intensity. "But I've known Albert since I was a child. He's like a brother to me."

"No better match than that of friends. And with the money Charles Maurice has ascertained through the Union Bridge Building Company, you'd never have to worry that Albert is marrying you for your money, which seems to be one of your major concerns. Is it not?" Mother's eyes narrowed to a most unladylike glare.

"I'm fairly certain Albert is interested in a girl named Eleanor. At least, that's what he told me last season." Hopefully, that was still the case. The last thing she wanted to do was hurt Albert's feelings.

"Poof." Mother's hand fanned the air. "Who could hold a candle to you? If only you would act upon the opportunities given you."

Savannah was tired of fighting with her mother all the time. It seemed they were at odds so often lately. There was no point in arguing that she felt nothing for Albert, or she'd get the same lecture on how her mother married her father to please her parents and yet they found love and compatibility together. "I assure you, if Albert was asking about me, he's merely inquiring as one of my few good friends on this island."

"Why must you be so difficult?"

"I'm not trying to be, Mother, but the endless tea parties and social obligations never seem to cease. I thought the time on this island was supposed to be more relaxed. I'm not even here twenty-four hours and I'm expected to—"

"Yes. You're expected to be polite. Is that too much to ask?"

"Of course not. I'll be sure and make my apologies to both Mrs. Maurice and Albert tonight at dinner. But can I please ask you for some consideration in allowing me to accept or decline my own social calendar? At least while we're on the island?" Savannah gave her mother the pleading look that normally melted her heart. "Please, Mama? You and Daddy always say the season at Jekyll is a time to be less formal and enjoy nature and relaxation."

The stern look on her mother's face gave way to a faint smile. "We do. But we must keep up appearances and not offend our dear friends."

"I will try to do better." Savannah moved forward and wrapped her arms around her mother's thin frame. Her stiff posture took a moment to relax. Daddy was much better at giving hugs.

Mother stepped back but laid her gloved hand on Savannah's cheek. "Your daddy and I just want you to find love and be as happy as we are."

A flash of Joseph's laughter and teasing banter came to mind. Now why would her brain instantly take her there? And why the uptick in her heartbeat at the mere thought of him? How terribly inconvenient. Mother would have a conniption at the thought of her falling for a lowly preacher. She would have to nip that one in the bud. And now.

Savannah turned toward the window and feigned interest in the view, though her heated cheeks might give her thoughts away. "I wish it was more acceptable for women to make it on their own if they desired. The same privilege men enjoy without question."

"That's not entirely accurate. Men care to be loved and have a family as much as women."

"I agree. But that is only one segment of their lives." Savannah turned back toward her mother. "They're also free to follow their dreams. Look at what Daddy's accomplished as a banker."

"Having a family, being a mother—since when are those things not accomplishments? I would've loved to have had more children, but it was not to be."

A sadness poured into her mother's eyes. The same look Savannah saw every time her mother spoke of children. She longed to find some words to ease the pain. "How many would you have liked?"

Mother came to stand beside Savannah. Her troubled expression spoke of dormant pain made fresh again. She gazed out the window toward the river with a blank stare. Her voice dropped to a mere whisper. "Charlotte Maurice birthed nine children, and I couldn't birth one."

"What?" Savannah's hand flew to her mouth. "I'm not...I'm not your daughter?"

CHAPTER 4

The window view, the bedroom, everything faded as Savannah stared at the woman she called Mother. She could not believe what she'd just heard.

Mother's head snapped up, and the daze she was in disappeared. "What do you mean by saying you're not my daughter?"

"But you said...you couldn't birth one."

Mother's spine popped into full starch mode. "I most certainly did not. I said that I could only have one. Whyever would you spout such nonsense?"

Savannah's head spun. She backed up until her knees found the edge of the bed and she sank down. "No, Mother. I heard—"

"You heard nothing of the kind. Your propensity for an overactive imagination has always been a problem." Her words were sharp and unyielding.

Savannah lifted a trembling hand to her temple and pressed against the instant headache. Her mother's voice had been soft, but there was nothing wrong with Savannah's ears.

"Don't make this into something, you hear me?"

"But if it's true, I'm old enough to know—"

"If what is true?"

Whenever her mother was not prepared to give an inch, she deflected by asking questions and projecting confusion. She was a master communicator and prided herself on the ability to both procure and possess information to her advantage.

Savannah shook her head. "It doesn't matter." She was not wrong about what she heard, but it was not her mother that would spill the truth. It would be her father. "I'm tired from traveling yesterday. If it's all right with you, I'd like to take a nap before dinner at seven."

"Yes, dear. Of course." Mother's hiked shoulders lowered, and she moved forward. "A rest seems in order. You're obviously not yourself. First, you miss an important engagement, and then you think you hear things that I never said." She dropped a light kiss on Savannah's forehead. With a flick of her wrist, she opened her gold watch hanging around her neck and looked at the time. "I'll send Emily up to wake you and help you dress for dinner in about an hour."

"Thank you."

The bedroom door closed softly behind the swish of her mother's fine silk gown.

Savannah dropped back onto the bed and pulled her legs up. She spread the light cotton blanket that lay at the end of her bed over her body and closed her eyes. Her tired frame curled into a fetal position. Sleep would not come. Her mother's words played over and over. *Charlotte Maurice birthed nine children, and I couldn't birth one.*

Her mother may not be ready for the truth, but so many little things over the years filtered in. Could it be possible Savannah was adopted? Her hands clenched and unclenched. That would mean she was not the bloodline of Henry and Anna Ensworth. A chill of concern spread through her bones. But then who was she? She must find out. Surely, Daddy wouldn't lie to her. But then again, he might not be her daddy.

~

The nonsensical chatter of the latest fashions from Paris, the popularizing of the Homburg hat that King Edward VII brought back from a town called Bad Homburg, Germany, and what Alexandra, his wife, wore at the latest ball bored Savannah senseless that evening. The Americans may have become independent of English rule but were certainly not free of what the fashion world in England and France dictated. It took every bit of Savannah's concentration to interject politely when appropriate.

Her gaze flicked around the dining room with its

carved oak woodwork, handcrafted wainscoting, high ceilings with textured beams, and gracefully arched entryway. Though considered simple compared to the opulence of most of the members' homes, the elegance could not be denied. Savannah viewed it through a different lens tonight.

She glanced to Joseph's table for the hundredth time that night. He had not been wrong when he bravely stated in his sermon that there was a need for the wealthy to wake up to the world around them and realize the disparaging difference between the haves and the have nots. But there he sat with Mr. George F. Baker, one of the wealthest men in the world. Oh to be close enough to hear that conversation.

Savannah was emotionally spent. She stifled a yawn behind her hand. Her day had begun with a startling attraction to not only the fine looks of the preacher, but what he was brave enough to stand for. Followed by the odd conversation with her mother. Savannah had no answers to the questions that roiled in her head. What possible good could come from knowing that her parents were not her biological mother and father? And then the tedious duty of dressing for dinner and playing the part society expected of her. Exhaustion pressed in.

Savannah gently placed the linen napkin on top of her barely touched plate of food. What a waste, if indeed Joseph's account was accurate and there were many without enough food to eat. That was not a problem in her world, nor a subject she had given any thought to. Until now.

The waiter pulled her plate away and set it on the tea trolley, then he returned with a dessert. She shook her head.

Aunt Mary's eyes pinned on the mousse in the waiter's hand. "Do bring that over here, young man. We can't have that going to waste." She laughed, causing the generous folds in her chin to jiggle and crease. She'd already finished every morsel on her own plate, *plus* dessert.

"Please excuse me, everyone," Savannah interjected before her aunt got going on her favorite subject of food. "With all the traveling in the last few days, I fear I must retire early."

They all nodded in understanding.

"I know what you mean." Aunt Mary lifted another spoonful of rich mousse just short of her lips. "I'll be right behind you, dearie, as soon as I'm done with your dessert. You don't know what you're missing. This is absolutely divine." The spoonful disappeared.

Savannah stood and pinched her shoulders back despite her fatigue. There was nothing her mother hated more than to compromise perfect posture. Heads turned as she wove her way gracefully to the exit. She was not unaccustomed to the attention but found it most wearisome. She didn't relax her shoulders until she was free of the dining room.

"Miss Ensworth."

Savannah heard her name but kept walking. All she wanted was a breath of fresh air before retiring to her room. Maybe if she moved quickly, she could avoid yet another conversation. She hurried out the door onto the veranda.

"Savannah."

Only a friend would use her first name, but she didn't recognize the voice. She whirled around. "Oh, Reverend, it's you."

"Joseph, please."

She made a conscious effort not to raise her eyebrows. He clearly didn't understand that one did not get that familiar so quickly.

"I see you're done with dinner. Might I interest you in an after-dinner stroll?"

"That would not be considered—"

"Ahh, but of course. I forget all the rules and regulations the gentry have. Or could it be that it is my station in life that makes a seemingly innocent walk in full view of the clubhouse unsuitable?"

"It is the fact that it's dark outside, and a woman's reputation relies heavily upon carefully chaperoned events."

"Oh, good. So it's not a slight against my invitation of friendship?"

"Goodness, no. I would hope I'm not as considerable a snob as that. But truth be told, I begged off before dessert because I'm genuinely tired from my travels. It would not look good to divert from my plan for an early night."

"Do you always care about what looks good and what does not?"

His pointed question rankled. He was far too forthright for her liking. Her chin lifted. "No, I'm not ruled by what others think, but I do try to remain honest, and if I said I was going to retire early, then I shall. I would think a man of the cloth would encourage one to be true to their word."

He laughed, a deep, rich rumble that set her heart to beating an erratic rhythm.

"I most assuredly do recommend you be a woman of your word. However, if I can arrange an afternoon on the beach tomorrow with Elizabeth and Walter along as chaperones, would you be agreeable to joining us?"

She could hear Elizabeth now...gloating at her match-making skills when friendship was all that was happening. But if Savannah set about winning the challenge, then Elizabeth would have no idea of the unsettling reactions this man indeed caused.

"Well?" He hit her with a dazzling smile.

His dancing dimples made her stomach flip. Gosh, she was standing there staring at him, with her mind blank to a usual sassy comeback. "I...ahh...yes, that would be agreeable."

His dark-gray eyes lit up in response. "Until then." He tipped his bowler and turned. His long legs took the steps from the clubhouse two at a time, and his frame retreated into the darkness.

She did not recognize the tune he whistled, but she stood there until the pleasant sound could no longer be heard.

CHAPTER 5

The trill of birdsong spilled through Savannah's open window. She stretched beneath the silky softness of her sheets. What was supposed to have been an early night and a restful slumber had been a collage of fitful snippets of sleep, troubled dreams, and many wide-awake moments tossing and turning.

Savannah pulled her body from the covers and sat on the edge of the bed. A faint light filtered in around the edges of the curtain. Morning had finally arrived, and she could not lie around one more minute. Normally, she found it hard to drag herself out of bed, but not today. Her father always rose early, and she hoped to join him on his morning walk around the compound.

With a rush in her step, she washed, struggled with the hook-and-eye clasps on her corset, and donned a pale-pink fine-cotton blouse with a navy gored skirt. She twisted her long hair into a loose bun at the nape of her neck and secured it with a few pins. She looked far from what her mother would approve as acceptable, but she had no patience to wait for Emily this morning. A walk with her father was what she needed to get answers to her troubling questions.

She knocked softly on the door of her parents' suite.

"Enter," her daddy's low baritone voice called out.

Savannah poked her head into the room. While her mother lay abed with her back turned, her handsome father sat in a chair by the window with a cup of tea. His eyes lit up in welcome. "Why, what a surprise. Come in, my dear."

Savannah shook her head and whispered so as not to wake her mother. "Are you just about ready for your morning walk? I thought I'd join you."

"That would be lovely."

"Knock on my door when you're done with your tea."

He nodded and she quietly exited. Mumbled voices caught her ear. She was not prone to eavesdropping, but the circumstances held her captive.

"That girl is rarely up early," Father observed.

Savannah pressed her ear closer. Clearly, her mother had not been sleeping.

"You know why she wants to go for a walk with you. Didn't you see her at supper last night? She barely spoke a word."

"I know."

"What are you going to tell her?" Her mother's voice wavered.

"How about the truth?"

"We cannot. Not after all these years. She'll think we've deceived her."

Savannah's heart dropped straight down to the soles of her walking boots. Her mother and father were not her biological parents.

Her mother continued, her voice low and urgent. "And what would those in our circle of friends think if Savannah could not keep this to herself and the truth leaked out? You know how she has a penchant for emotionalism."

Far better that way than to be as constrained and controlled as her mother.

"She has a right to know." Daddy spoke firmly.

"Why? We're her parents. I'm her mother in every way that counts, and you're her father. What earthly good could it do to upset that truth? Besides, if this leaked out, all of Savannah's chances for a well-appointed marriage would fly out the window. You know how elitist our circle of friends can be."

"I do." Daddy's voice had dropped.

Savannah pulled her ear from the door at the sound of movement. She barely made it back into her room and closed her door before her parents' door clicked open. She took a deep breath in and slowly out.

The short rap made her jump. If only she had more

time to process the startling news before seeing her daddy's face. Would she be able to feign ignorance? She had never completely perfected masking her emotions. She was more prone to speak her mind, much to her mother's chagrin.

She opened the door to the man she absolutely adored. His fit physique from all the walking he did and the fact he preferred vegetables to rich delicacies took years off his age. He also refused to smoke cigars like most of his contemporaries, believing that no good could come from inhaling smoke. Distinguished gray peppered the hair on his temples and thick walrus mustache. His smile was strained.

Savannah slipped out the door to join him. Her heart hammered against her chest. Her world as she knew it was caving in. If she was not this dear man's daughter, who was she?

"Looks like another beautiful day."

Savannah nodded, too tongue tied to respond.

They walked into the balmy morning, so different from the bitter cold of a New York winter. Birdsong filled the air, and the sun gained strength in the eastern sky. All was as it should be except for a nagging truth that could change everything…if she spoke up.

No. She didn't want to know. They didn't want to tell her, and she wouldn't push for information. But could she pretend she'd never heard her mother's words the day before or stood by their bedroom door and listened in? Yes. She could and would do it. They turned onto

Shell Road and began the loop around the fenced enclosure. Savannah was thankful for the protection. She had seen how a wild boar had gored one of the guests when hunting and had no aspirations to encounter one.

"You're unusually quiet." Father's voice broke through her reverie.

"You know me. I'm not a fan of this island. It has a way of allowing way too much time to think. I'd rather be busy."

"Without these few months of relaxation, golfing, fishing, and walking along the beach, I don't think I could go at the pace I have to the rest of the year."

"Do you enjoy your work?" Savannah slipped her hand into the crook of his arm. As they turned toward the river, the smell of sea salt and tidal marshlands blew in on a soft breeze. She drew in a deep breath. The air was indeed sweeter than that in the streets of downtown New York City.

"Banking is not for the faint of heart. Especially at my level. George Baker is a good friend, but he's also a man who demands excellence. The First National Bank did not get to where it is today without constantly adapting to changing times."

"Now if only they would change enough to let a woman take over, then I could step in when the time comes." Savannah lifted her chin and sent him a look of challenge. "Had I been your son and not a daughter, they wouldn't think twice of inviting me to apprentice beside you."

"You are more than intelligent enough. But that would take quite the change. Your best chance in life is to marry well and find a strong man who is not threatened by the strong woman you are—"

"Daddy, can we please not have the *marriage* discussion yet again?"

Silence fell between them. They turned onto River Road and strolled past the row of cottages.

"Looks as though the Goodyear Cottage is almost done." Daddy pointed to the new white-stucco cottage with a line of scalloped corbels beneath the roof overhang and rows of large generous windows on all sides of the house. "Frank and Josephine will have all the privacy they want. I couldn't be bothered with building and maintaining another home. The clubhouse works for me."

Savannah leaned her head on his strong shoulder. "Thanks for changing the subject, and I shouldn't have so rudely cut you off. It's just that marriage scares me. If a woman doesn't choose well, every bit of freedom will be gone."

"You'll be surprised how much power a woman can brandish. Look at your mother. She says jump, and I ask how high." He chuckled.

"You're an amazing father and husband. But I think you're one of a kind. The men I meet are so self-centered, spoiled, entitled—"

"And you see none of those qualities in yourself?"

"Daddy." She pulled away enough to slap his arm. "And here I thought you deemed me perfect."

"I do, darling. I do. But we all have our weaknesses and our strengths. You refuse to give any young man a fair shake."

"I've yet to find one that deserves a chance."

Joseph's face instantly swam into view. How annoying to think of him as someone deserving. His sermon on how all humanity was equal in the eyes of God had been spoken with such authority and intelligence, yet with a kindness that haunted the portals of her mind. And who could dismiss those gunmetal eyes which twinkled above laughing dimples and a charming smile? There would be no bigger disappointment to her parents' plan than for her to fall for a lowly preacher.

"Daddy?"

His "yes?" sounded reluctant.

"What do you think of God? I mean, do you think there is one?"

Daddy smoothed a hand over his moustache. "Hmm, that is a deep question for so early in the morning. I suppose I believe that something bigger than me had to create all this beauty." His strong hand swept out toward the river. "When I'm on this island, close to nature, I have to admit I feel something. Why do you ask?"

"I went to church yesterday because Elizabeth

invited me. There's this preacher who speaks very differently than anyone I've heard before."

"Yes. There was quite the discussion in the drawing room last evening. Seems the young man ruffled a few feathers in his straight-forward ignorance. He has much to learn."

"Does he?" Savannah threw her father a glance. "Or is it the rest of us who have much to learn?"

"What do you mean by that?" Daddy stopped walking. "This young whippersnapper comes along and reprimands the very ones who put food on his table. I'm sure his father will not be happy to hear of his insolence."

Savannah turned toward him. "But he just read out of the Bible...the words of Jesus. Something about it being easier for a camel to go through the eye of a needle than for a rich man to enter the kingdom of heaven. Is that really in the Bible?"

"Of course, it's not. The young man was showboating. How could a camel go through the eye of a needle, anyway? That's impossible." He started walking. Agitation flowed from the clipped pace of each step.

"I think that was his point." Savannah increased her pace to match his. "Maybe with all our money, we fail to see the need around us, and Jesus apparently demands we help the poor."

"We do our part. Your mother is involved in all kinds of charities, and I donate generously to more than you know."

"And that's enough?"

"Of course it is, darling. Don't take that man too seriously. I work hard for my money, and I've invested wisely. I don't think God can take credit for that, or demand how I spend it, now, can He?"

"I suppose not." Savannah ducked her head under a long strand of silver Spanish moss that dangled from the twisted limb of a live oak. There was something about their majestic, ancient presence that begged her to consider more than the tea parties, charity dances, and endless social engagements she endured.

"Come on now." Daddy threw his arm around her shoulder. "Where's that smile? You've been much too morose as of late. You're young. You're beautiful. You have every opportunity this life can afford. And your daddy loves you more than words can say."

Savannah lifted her head to the warm, lemony sunlight brushing the tips of the trees and threw a generous smile his way. "You're right."

CHAPTER 6

Joseph had never felt so excited about a friendship before. He headed down the narrow steps from the servants' quarters on the fourth floor of the clubhouse, shaking his head at how the opulence improved and the steps got wider on the floors where guests occupied the space. Apparently, the servants that these wealthy millionaires brought along to serve them did not merit the added safety. That noticeable difference rankled, but he shook it off. One sermon at a time.

For today, he planned to have a wonderful afternoon with his good friends, Elizabeth and Walter, and his new friend, Savannah. He had no wish to complicate a perfect afternoon with sermon material.

He hurried past the boar's head hanging over the fireplace in the foyer, deliberately avoiding eye contact. Every time he went by, he swore that the eyes on that thing followed him. A hunter he was not. The thought of shooting any of God's creatures did not appeal to him in the least. He burst through the main door a little too quickly and almost sent a lady flying. His arm shot out to steady her. "Please, forgive me."

She backed up with a huff and pulled her arm free. "Young people these days. Always in a hurry." Her nose went up in the air, and she stomped forward, barking out an order. "Kenneth, get the door." The valet beside her hopped into action.

Joseph slowed across the broad veranda but took the steps two at a time. As they waited in the shade of a nearby live oak, Walter had a grin on his face and Elizabeth's green eyes sparkled with her laughter.

"You're not at the races, my friend." Walter gave his back a hearty slap. "People move slowly on this island."

"So I see."

"That was Mrs. Louisa Morgan. You do not want to get on the wrong side of her. Her husband, J.P. Morgan, is a founder of this club and one of the wealthiest men in the world."

Joseph longed to spew out how unimpressed he was by that, but he held his tongue. Best not to alienate a good friend. "I'll have to pay a bit more mind."

"I wonder if Savannah has decided not to show." Walter scanned the veranda.

"Oh, she's coming. I spoke with her at breakfast." Elizabeth's expressive eyes sparkled with mischief.

What did she know that Joseph did not?

"Are you ready?" a soft voice whispered from behind him.

Joseph whirled around. His gaze swept Savannah from head to toe.

She wore a white skirt of light material that floated to her ankles over a sleeveless swimsuit with a black-and-white sailor-style collar. The swooping neckline hugged her figure in a way he dared not feast his eyes upon, so he cast them downward. They landed on a pair of shapely legs that the light skirt with sunlight streaming through did little to hide. He was in way over his head. Nothing about the thundering of his heart resembled friendship.

"Savannah, that matching ensemble looks amazing. Wherever did you find it?" Elizabeth asked.

"Mother's new seamstress assured her this is what all the young women are wearing, so you know Mother —she had it made for me." Savannah twirled in a graceful circle.

Joseph had to do something to distract himself. He turned to Walter. "Do you think it'll be warm enough to swim?"

"It's unseasonably warm. But most likely we'll just dip our toes in."

"Good. Then I won't bother changing. I'll just roll up my trousers."

"You struck me as one of those men who would be first into the surf." Savannah arched a dainty brow. "And I was going to race you."

The thought of the two of them frolicking in the water sent a heated rush to his face. Was she flirting with him? Didn't they make it clear there would be none of that? If only his heart agreed.

"I do love swimming, but—"

"Let's go." Walter waved his hand toward a shiny black Oldsmobile. "Father let me use his prized possession. Of course, I got the sermon not to go faster than six miles an hour, and to make sure I stop to the oncoming horse-drawn carriages. All of which we won't have to worry about once we get to the beach and have some wide-open space. We'll rev it up and see how fast she can fly."

"You'll leave me safely on the beach before you try that, thank you very much." Elizabeth's hands planted firmly on both sides of her hips.

But Savannah's dark-brown eyes lit up, and Joseph looked away so as not to be mesmerized.

"I'm game," Joseph said at the exact same time as Savannah. They turned to each other and laughed.

Elizabeth shook her head at Savannah. "Oh, you would be. I don't know how two more opposite people than us could become friends."

Savannah threw her arm around Elizabeth's shoulder as they walked to the shiny car with spoked wheels. "You know I love you." She giggled.

Joseph's pulse bolted at the sound of those words strung together. What would it be like to look into her dark-brown eyes and hear her say those words to him?

What was wrong with him? Their worlds were as far apart as any could be. He had to stop such nonsensical thoughts.

He took one look at the car with only one bench seat and made a swift decision. "There's certainly not room for four on that seat. I'll grab a bike and meet you there."

"Thought Savannah could sit on your knee." Walter winked as if there was some hidden message between them, as though they had discussed such an improper possibility. Why did he do that? The unwanted heat rushed to Joseph's face.

"I definitely want a ride at the beach, but I'm sure the ladies would much prefer a little comfort. Besides, I'll probably beat you there. Those autos are known to break down more than they work."

Savannah threw him a saucy look. "I do believe the good reverend protests too much."

Now what did she mean by that?

The three of them laughed as the automobile chugged away. Savannah turned back and waved.

A collision happened—his heart against the wall of his chest.

CHAPTER 7

The one-mile ride down Shell Road was exhilarating. Savannah could not get enough speed. She knew what her next birthday request would be. Why should men have all the fun?

From semi-tropical growth of oak, magnolia, palmetto, and cedar, the road cut between some sand dunes and opened to a wide section of hard-packed sand. The expanse of the Atlantic Ocean spread before them in all its glory. Walter drove out onto the sand and cut the motor.

Savannah inhaled a deep breath. The clean smell of sea salt filled her nostrils. She closed her eyes to better savor the rhythmic, soft cadence of low-tide waves gently slapping the shoreline. The ocean drew her, and she slipped from the automobile and took in the vista.

"So you're going to go through with this?" Elizabeth

whispered. "That most definitely was the Savannah charm I saw at work back there."

"It should be fun." Savannah giggled.

"Maybe it's not such a good idea."

"What are you ladies whispering about?" Walter leaned back in the seat of his newest toy like a proud papa.

"The sea and sand are down here, my love." Elizabeth skillfully avoided his question.

"You two go ahead and enjoy. I'm quite content to bask in the sun right where I am until Joseph gets here."

"We'll dip our toes in." Savannah linked her arm with Elizabeth's and pulled her toward the water.

"Why the concern all of a sudden?"

"I've had time to think, and it seems kind of callous. He's Walter's friend, after all."

"This was your idea."

"I know. I wanted you to meet him because you both had the same *I'll never marry* attitude. I thought you deserved each other. But now..."

"Oh, come on, Elizabeth, he's only here for the month. What harm can come?" She raised her hand to her hat, holding it in place against the tug of the wind. "Quite frankly, it's refreshing to spend time with someone who is not so predictable. The men in our circles are all so dreadfully tiresome, but I can't say that about the good reverend. It will be fun to see if I can get him to love me as much as that Jesus of his."

"And what if he does fall for you?"

"Then he shall have a great memory for when he's old and gray, sitting on a porch somewhere with his boring Bible."

"I'm not only concerned about him."

Savannah turned to face her friend. "What? You think I'm going to succumb to his charms?"

"What if you do?" Elizabeth's voice drifted away in the wind. "I'd feel terrible, because it could never work."

"And you think I don't know that?"

"You do, but you're stubborn enough to rock the boat, and his boat can't be rocked. You would never make a preacher's wife, and he would never fit into your world. I don't want that on my conscience."

Savannah threw back her head and laughed. "All right, I'll tone down the flirting and invest in friendship. Got any objections to that?"

"No. Friendship is good. Speaking of which...here he comes."

Savannah looked back toward the tree line. True to his word, Joseph was not long behind them. They had stopped three different times to allow a horse and buggy to pass by. And there he was, riding like the wind across the sand. The breeze had whipped his shirt open, corded muscles bugling beneath his rolled-up sleeves. With his bronzed skin and those dimples, there wasn't much *not* to like. Now why couldn't she find a man in her circles that stirred her blood as much as the one speeding toward her?

He stopped the bike with a skid in front of them, spraying the sand like a young boy. His zest for life was infectious.

"Walter's going to show me how to drive the automobile, and then I'll come back and take you for a joyride. If you're willing?" He looked directly at Savannah with a challenge in his eyes.

"Absolutely." She pushed down the butterflies fluttering in her stomach that had nothing to do with the danger of the ride and everything to do with the man.

"Thought you might." He gave her a dashing smile and headed back to the automobile.

"See, that's what I mean." Elizabeth nudged her arm. "I'm terrified of that machine, and Walter knows what he's doing. But you...you're completely all right with joining a novice for a ride. You're perfect for each other."

"Oh stop. Let's get our feet wet and enjoy the moment."

Savannah frolicked in the waves, keeping an eye on the driving lessons. Joseph was a natural. When he motioned her over, she was more than ready.

"Wind, wild, and wonderful. Want to join me?" Joseph patted the seat beside him. Walter hopped down and gave Savannah his arm. She didn't need help and would've ignored the gesture but didn't want to hurt his feelings.

"Have fun," Walter yelled as they drove off.

Savannah lifted the hat from her head and placed it

on her lap. The breeze whipped through her hair as their speed increased. Nothing but wide-open sand lay before them, and Savannah laughed into the wind. She pulled out the few remaining pins that tugged to confine her thick hair with one hand and held onto the seat with the other. The freedom brought tears to her eyes. If only every moment could feel so unfettered.

The wheels bumped over a small sand dune, and she grabbed at Joseph's arm.

He took his eyes from the sand to grin down at her. "We're going as fast as she goes. Are you scared?"

"Never."

He laughed. "Didn't think so." They drove for a few minutes in silence. The blend of sand, sea, and sky mixed with a splash of speed brought exhilaration to her soul. Or was it the man sitting beside her? She had not had this much fun in a very long time. She wasn't scared, but she held onto his arm, anyway. The feel of his sinewy strength beneath her fingers sent a quiver up her arm.

Joseph slowed the automobile down to the speed they had been forced to drive on Shell Road and turned the vehicle back in the direction they came. "I guess there are some perks to being wealthy. I could get used to this."

"I know what I'm going to ask Daddy for for my next birthday."

"And you'll get it?"

"Oh, he'll balk." She flicked a lock of hair away from

her face. "And I'll have to convince him that a woman can operate a machine as well as a man. But I'll get it."

"So confident."

"It's what Daddy taught me to be. It's his fault."

Joseph laughed.

Savannah loved the deep rumble of his laughter.

"Well, I'd certainly teach you how to drive this, but it's not my automobile."

"That's progressive of you. But I fear Walter's dad is very old-fashioned. He wouldn't think a woman could handle any such adventure."

"I agree. He is, rather. But his wife, now she's a firecracker and a lot of fun." He grinned at her. "I guess the adage that opposites attract is true."

It was such an odd friendship, this young preacher and Walter. "How do you know the Nielsen family so well?"

"Our fathers go way back. My father is a well-known Presbyterian reverend in New York City, and Walter's dad is a long-time member of that church. Mr. Nielsen senior has a lot of money, as you well know, and in my father's world, money talks. He gives special attention and devoted friendship to those who generously give to his church."

"And money doesn't talk in your world?"

"No. That's why my father and I butt heads so much. He convinced Mr. Nielsen to ask the powers that be to substitute me in his place here on this island with an ulterior motive. He wants me to experience first-hand the benefits of the wealthy and the advantage of rubbing shoulders with them."

"Is that what you're doing with me?" Savannah leaned into his arm and gave a nudge. Shocking, how comfortable and bold she was with him. His genuineness drew her in.

"I think you know that's not the case. My request for friendship is sincere, and I do want to understand more about your lifestyle. I see both the challenges and privileges that Walter experiences, but it's different for women. They seem to be an extension of their husband's wishes rather than an equal partner."

"Equal partner. I like the sound of that. That is certainly not what most men in my social circle think. We're more a decoration on their arm. A status symbol dressed in the finest to parade their wealth."

Joseph gave her a quick frown before pinning his eyes back on the sand in front of them. "So you don't think that if you got married, the wealth would be shared, as much yours as it is his?"

"Absolutely not. Even if a man married into my money, he would assume control. Why do you think I resist marriage so adamantly?"

"You do?" His eyebrows lifted. "Under all circumstances?"

"Can't think of a scenario that would make a difference."

"How about marrying for love? Surely, if a man loves you, he'd respect you as an equal."

"Hmm, love." She nodded her head. "It would make marriage tolerable. I can tell my father truly loves my mother and she's content. I just want more than her." She threw her arms open wide. Her hat gripped between her fingers whipped in the wind, shedding the fake flower petals. "I want to learn and create, and follow whatever dream takes my fancy, not be bound only by things a woman is traditionally supposed to do."

"I know women may have different roles in a marriage than men, but each are equally important. And quite frankly, women should be able to achieve whatever goals they wish."

Savannah looked out toward the ocean. "See all that water, Joseph?"

He nodded.

"You're like one tiny drop in that body of water, with the rest being the number of men who believe differently than you. Where did you get such open-minded thinking?"

"The Bible."

Savannah turned her head to him and laughed. "The Bible?"

"Yes, the Bible."

His lopsided grin with accompanying dimples sent a thrill up her spine.

"It says in Galatians that 'there is neither Jew nor Greek, neither slave nor free, neither male nor female; for we are all one in Christ Jesus.' Meaning that if Jesus doesn't make a distinction and sees us all the same, how can I?"

"So you're in favor of the suffrage movement?"

"Absolutely. I don't understand why women don't have the same right as men to vote. Honestly, I've met some far more intelligent women than a lot of men I know, and yet, in my opinion, the lesser of the two is the one casting the vote."

Savannah had tried many times to have this conversation with the men in her circle of friends, and each one had patted her hand condescendingly and tried to change the subject. Joseph, on the other hand, with his Jesus and his dimples, completely threw off her equilibrium. She didn't have a response to such an amazing observation.

He leaned in close as he slowed the automobile to a stop at the place they'd started. "Cat got your tongue, pretty lady?"

She looked up into his laughing blue-gray eyes that darkened to smoky slate as he held her gaze. "If your Jesus advocates equality, I'm that much more intrigued."

"That's good. I hope to inspire you to love Jesus as much as I do."

Little did he know, when she mentioned being intrigued, it was not in his Jesus, but in him. Why did the first man she could finally have an intelligent conversation with be one her parents would never approve of?

CHAPTER 8

One week bled into two, and Savannah pinched herself to be sure she was not dreaming. She enjoyed her daily interaction with Joseph more than she would admit. Boredom was no longer in her vocabulary. They rode bikes, walked for miles along the seashore, and she had even taken to teaching him how to play tennis. All within the properity of Elizabeth and Walter in the mix.

She lifted a cup of tea to her lips as she gazed out the window of the clubhouse dining room. Everything on the island looked different. Joseph continually pointed out the flora and fauna, the different shapes of clouds in the sky, the sound of birdsong, or his favorite —the sound of waves. He told her that in the book of Ezekiel there was a verse that said the sound of God's voice was like many waters. She smiled to herself. Of course, Joseph had gone on and on about how much he loved the sound of water, from a bubbling brook to the lap of waves upon a lakeshore, to the crashing breakers of the ocean or a thundering waterfall.

"What has you smiling so pretty this early in the morning?"

Savannah gave a little start. Albert Maurice stood at her table. Her happy musings had made her blind to his approach.

"May I?"

She nodded, and he pulled out a chair and slid onto the seat.

"Haven't seen much of you yet this season. You're usually so bored and begging me to find a way to curb the tedium."

Savannah pasted on her perfect smile, the practised one that barely turned up the corners of her mouth. "'Tis true, but not this year."

"Could it be that a certain preacher has caught your eye?"

Savannah's heartbeat kicked up speed. Were people noticing? She laughed and flapped her napkin at him. "Don't be silly, Albert."

"Not so silly. Everyone who is anyone is talking about how much time the two of you are spending together."

"What? That's preposterous. I'm duly chaperoned at all times. And Joseph is a perfect gentleman."

"See, even the way you say his name gives it away to those who know you as well as I do."

"Gives what away?" Savannah worked hard to keep her expression flat.

"Savannah. How long have we been friends? We've been confiding in each other since we were ten." "Joseph just so happens to be a good friend of Walter and Elizabeth, so what am I to do? Be a snob?"

"No argument from me." He reached across the table and gave her hand a light squeeze. "But as a friend, I thought you should know there is a fair amount of gossip circulating. I can't believe your parents haven't said anything to you."

They had, but Savannah had shot them down. She was a gifted mitigator. The argument had fizzled when she'd accused them of being double-minded. How they had fought for the freedom of black people from slavery, something they were indeed proud of, but would not allow her to befriend someone from a lower social standing. When she'd assured them she was no more than friends with Joseph and reminded them he'd soon be gone, they'd dropped the subject completely.

"My parents are well aware of my friendship, and that's all it is, Albert. Maybe as my long-time friend, you can spread that little ditty."

"I have been. I know you, Savannah. The last thing you'd ever want is to be is tied down by religion or become a preacher's wife."

Savannah bit her lower lip to still the barrage of words that ached to spill out on Joseph's behalf. He was proving to be far more upright and interesting than any man she had ever met...a man with deep layers of intelligence and compassion. And his faith was so much more than religion. It flowed from his being in a natural, infectious way, a way she longed to understand. But how could she begin to explain this to Albert? "Who said anything about becoming his wife? You and I are great friends, but that doesn't mean wedding bells are in our future."

"I know, and between you and me..." He leaned across the table. "I'm quite taken with Eleanor."

"That's what I thought. Now if someone would please tell my mother that." Savannah laughed. "She seems to think I should be spending more time with you."

"Oh no, you're way too much woman for me. I pity the man who finally tames you enough to slip a ring on your finger."

"Ouch. I could be offended by that." Savannah lifted her chin and her brows.

"But you're not. You're as tough as a crocodile hide, and that's the way you like it."

Heat rose in her cheeks. Was she prickly? It wasn't how she wanted to be, but when things did not seem right or fair, she was not afraid to speak up. "Am I really that unbearable?" Savannah's lower lip formed a pout.

"You're authentic, and I wouldn't have you any other way." Albert stood. "Just thought as a friend I would let you know what the season's tidings are heralding, and it has nothing to do with angels and baby Jesus." He leaned close enough to whisper in her ear. "But your eyes do light up at the mention of his name. You best work on that if you want to fool me." He pulled back with a smile on his face. "See you in church."

Savannah had a childish urge to stick her tongue out at him as he walked away, but that would not be ladylike. As Albert turned through the doorway, she caught Joseph staring at her from a table across the room. Instant shivers skimmed over her flesh, and she lifted her hand in a tiny wave.

The corners of his mouth held a sad smile. He nodded ever so slightly and looked away. Try as she might, she couldn't get his attention the rest of her breakfast. Was he ignoring her?

∽

Joseph scanned the congregation from the pulpit. His gaze landed on Savannah in her soft-pink dress, with her beautiful, upswept hair and rich brown eyes. He quickly looked away.

He was here to work. Give of himself to the Lord. And one very attractive, interesting woman was stealing his attention. He stood behind the wooden pulpit, the congregation waiting for his instruction, but his concentration was gone.

All he could think about was how perfect Albert Maurice and Savannah had looked together earlier that morning. The same breeding, culture, money...a match that made sense in most every way. Yet the sin of jealousy had lifted its ugly head as he watched the two of them together, so comfortable and cozy. The way Albert had touched her hand, her laughing banter in return, then the secret they'd shared so intimately before he walked away.

He bowed his head. "Let us open in prayer." He was the one who needed prayer. An awkward silence filled the room as all heads bowed. When the Spirit urged him to ask Bernice to pray, he did so without second guessing. Yet the sweet older lady whom he knew loved the Lord with all her heart remained silent.

He glanced up. She sat in the front row. Her eyes bulged in fear. He nodded at her to proceed, though he understood it was unheard of to ask a woman to lead in prayer. But God saw them all the same. He needed a strong believer to pray for the service this morning, and she was the one.

The Holy Spirit was not wrong. A calm came over him as her sweet voice filled the chapel. Her voice and prayer gained strength as she allowed the Spirit to take over. Joseph took a deep breath in and let it slowly out. By the time she was done praying, he was ready.

With a smile, he began. His message on the true meaning of Christmas poured out of him. His shoulders slowly relaxed, and he unclenched his one hand that had been clutching his notes so tightly they were crumpled in one corner. He was able to scan the room, look into the eyes of many, even Savannah, without losing concentration. God was good. The strength came to speak even that which was tough.

He took a deep breath as he made his way to the doorway to shake peoples' hands as they filtered out. There were many who voiced their approval but some who walked straight by without a glance. It was to be expected.

Savannah waited in line. His heart hammered against his ears. She reached out a gloved hand, hers so delicate inside the strength and size of his.

She leaned her head close. "We'll have to discuss this sermon later. I have some troubling questions." Her eyebrows arched over widened eyes. "I'll see you this afternoon, won't I?"

He had avoided her the past few days with every excuse he could think of to be busy. His control was slipping, and he was falling in love with everything about her. He croaked out a response. "Yes."

She drew her hand free and turned away. His gaze followed her down the path. Her shoulders sagged, and her head was down, so very unlike the Savannah he had come to know.

CHAPTER 9

Savannah stood on the fringe of the group. The afternoon garden tea at the Gould's Chicota Cottage was one of the responsibilities she had to endure for propriety's sake. All she wanted was to be free of this obligation so she could have a conversation with Joseph.

His message this morning had not only made her uncomfortable, but the others were talking as well.

"Can you believe the impudence?" Sarah asked. "As if he understands our lifestyle."

Heads nodded in agreement.

"I never expected to be reproved so severely, and in church, no less." Aunt Mary wafted her burning red cheeks with a fan that looked like a palmetto branch. "As if I'm not hot and bothered enough at this stage of life." The wicker chair creaked as she shifted her large bottom, and the wrinkles on her forehead increased in number. Her double chin turned into a triple as she harrumphed. "The nerve of that commoner telling us how things need to be done."

"Who contracted him, anyway? And why is he here for more than the allotted two weeks?" Mrs. Hoffman asked.

Mrs. Gould sat quietly at a table sipping her iced tea. Her large hat with colorful spring flowers and scalloped edges shadowed her face. She looked the picture of serenity. "Ladies, you must taste this latest brew." She held up her glass. "Tea that is iced, no less. I first tried it at the St. Louis World Fair two years ago, and I think my staff have finally mastered it."

"Iced, you say? I could use something cold right now." Aunt Mary's fan picked up speed.

Savannah smiled. Mrs. Gould had successfully turned the topic to pleasantries, as only a gifted hostess could do. But Savannah had to get a moment alone with Joseph. She had to warn him. He was making more enemies than friends.

Savannah slipped into a chair next to her mother. "Have I been here long enough to make a polite departure?" she whispered.

"Why? So you can run off with you-know-who?" Her mother's voice dropped down to a whisper as well. "Can't you see how ill-fitting that friendship is?"

"I have a tennis match planned, and you know how long it takes to get out of all these layers."

"And who are you playing with?"

"Elizabeth."

"And?"

Savannah knew exactly what her mother was asking without spelling it out for others to overhear.

"And Walter." Savannah dropped a kiss on her cheek and faced her hostess. "Thank you, Mrs. Gould, for your lovely hospitality. And if you are sharing the secret, I would love the recipe to that iced tea of yours. It was so refreshing compared to hot tea on a warm day like this."

Mrs. Gould nodded graciously.

Savannah turned to Mrs. Gould's daughter. "And Sarah, thank you for the invitation."

A rather flat grin played on Sarah's lips, and she dipped her head ever so slightly. Judging by that look, the invitation had been all Mrs. Gould's idea.

"Now if you'll excuse me, ladies, I have a tennis match to win." Savannah smiled. Her cheeks aching from the past two hours of forcing her lips upward. "You all know the rules for punctuality on the courts. I mustn't be late."

She walked with grace through the grouping of tables over the cloth ground cover that had been put down to preserve the hems of their dresses. It took every bit of control to take her time and say a few polite words to every lady on her way.

Tommy, one of the livery staff who waited to escort the ladies back to the clubhouse, helped her up into the carriage. Savannah kept her posture ramrod straight, just as mother had trained her. It was not until they were out of sight that she let her back relax into the cushions.

She was not at all interested in the tennis game, but the man she needed to speak to would be there. Her pulse accelerated, and a wash of heat that had nothing to do with the warm weather spilled over her. There was no point any longer in denying the powerful emotions that surged within her at the mere thought of Joseph Bennett. What Elizabeth had been afraid would happen…was happening.

~

Savannah had one of the worst tennis games in a very long time. Usually she was hard to beat, but today her mind was elsewhere.

"Are you throwing the game just to make me feel good?" Joseph yelled from the other side of the court.

Elizabeth poked her with her racket. "Yeah, Savannah, what's your problem? The two of us girls should be severely crushing these gentlemen, and the game is forty-love."

They all approached the net.

"Not much into it today," Savannah said. "I have a bit of a headache." She pressed her temple with her free hand.

"Since I'm abysmal at the game all of the time…"

Joseph laughed. "Why don't Savannah and I sit this one out and watch you two experts play?"

That was music to Savannah's ears. "Great idea." She immediately made her way to the bench, and Joseph joined her.

"I was hoping to have the opportunity to speak to you, anyway." Savannah set her racket on the bench beside her.

"What's bothering you? Clearly, your head was not in that game. And you seemed troubled when you left the church this morning."

"Yes." Savannah nodded but didn't know how to begin. Silence hung between them like a dark cloud, but Joseph waited like a gentleman and didn't pressure her. "That sermon this morning. It...well, it was...it was..."

He turned toward her. "Savannah, you can be honest with me." He gave her hand a quick squeeze.

A rush of awareness scuttled up her arm, and she lost her train of thought.

"What is it?" Concern filled his kind eyes.

"It was rude, and bold, and ever so uncomfortable. And you should have heard the ladies at the tea this afternoon. They were offended, and some even angry."

"The Word of God has a way of doing that. It's described in the Bible as being living and powerful, sharper than a double-edged sword."

"Stop, Joseph." She held up both hands.

"Stop what?" A troubled look stole into his eyes.

Savannah let out a huff. "Stop with the riddles, the camel going through the eye of a needle and the double-edged sword...and all that nonsense. Just explain why you would tell those good people they are not doing enough. You don't know what charities they give to. You don't know their hearts. You're not the judicator and the jury."

His hand rubbed across his forehead. "No, but I am a shepherd, and a good shepherd will always tend his sheep."

"There you go again, with more riddles. You're not a shepherd. You are a young preacher who is offending the flock—if you must use the shepherd metaphor."

"If you noticed, I used Scripture. Those were not my words, but the words of Jesus. And there were religious people in that day who did not appreciate Him, either, so much so that they crucified Him."

Savannah threw her hands up. "It's Christmas in two weeks. Why can't you stick to baby Jesus in a manger?"

"But I did—"

"Yes, you started off well, with angels singing glory to God in the highest, and wise men visiting and giving gifts, but then suddenly, the baby Jesus was an adult preaching a story of a widow who gave her all and the wealthy only giving a pittance out of their abundance."

"Yes, but I brought that back to how we, like the angels and wise men, can give glory to God by our actions, by our giving, by our—"

"Don't you see how pointed that is? How arrogant?"

"But Savannah, the wealthy have opportunities to do such great things, to help so many hurting people. Should I not be encouraging that, even prodding if necessary?"

Savannah lifted her chin and looked out at Elizabeth and Walter hitting the ball back and forth. "It's not your place."

"I'm a preacher. If it's not my place, whose place is it?"

"The church they belong to back home...when they're not on holidays trying to enjoy themselves."

Joseph fell silent, so quiet that Savannah chanced a peek. Lines furrowed his forehead. His gunmetal eyes smoldered like blue flames staring right through her.

"I pray I do not come across as arrogant. I agonized over the message the Holy Spirit gave me. It was not an easy step of obedience."

Savannah shook her head. She didn't understand this obedience thing. It all sounded too personal. She much preferred God from a distance. "Church used to be boring, but with you, it's even worse."

Joseph's eyebrows lifted.

"It's so uncomfortable. And I have to agree with the consensus...your messages are totally inappropriate for a traveling preacher."

"Don't you think I would like to tickle the ears with stories of baby Jesus? And pat the backs of this country's most wealthy with platitudes of how wonderful they are, instead of speaking honestly? I know this will filter back to my father and he, too, will be livid."

Savannah turned to him. She desperately wanted to help him and his career. "Then why do it?"

"I must follow Jesus first."

"Jesus." Savannah spat the word out and stood. "Then you leave me no choice. Our friendship...or whatever this is. I just can't..." She turned and walked away.

"Savannah." Her name ripped from his lips.

She kept on walking.

CHAPTER 10

A heaviness settled in. Savannah hurried past the clubhouse toward the river. She didn't care that she was in her tennis attire and etiquette would demand she change. The briskness in her step matched the churning of her soul. The bench where she'd first met Joseph came into view. She headed that way and sank down. That meeting seemed like months ago, when in reality, it had only been two weeks. They had crammed a lot of laughter, fun, and deep conversations into a small amount of time.

Never had she met anyone like him. A man who could make her laugh so effortlessly, cause her to observe things she had missed, and touch the deepest part of her heart. The loss of his friendship was palpable.

She leaned her head back and closed her eyes. A

heavy sigh slipped from her lips. How would she find the strength to ignore him until he was gone?

"Seems we both had the same idea." At Joseph's voice, her eyes snapped open. "I can leave. I thought you went into the clubhouse to change, and I needed some solitude—"

"So did I."

"I'll go." He turned.

"Wait." Savannah heard her own voice but had no idea why or what she wanted to say.

He turned back and stared at her. Fresh pain darkened his eyes.

A pang of remorse knocked on the door of her heart. Why was she punishing him for doing his job, for listening to his Jesus, for following a deep conviction when most of the men in her life only followed after pleasure?

"I'm sorry..."

They both spoke the words at the same time—once again, in each other's head. They had a connection unlike anything she had experienced before.

"Ladies first. May I sit?" He pointed to the bench beside her.

She nodded. Her good intentions turned to sawdust. She could not ignore those soulful eyes. The bench groaned under the weight of his six-foot frame, but she kept her eyes focused on the water in front of her.

"Truth be told, your sermons prick my conscience. They make me feel...self-centered. I've honestly never given thought to what a servant or a black man or woman would feel." A tear slipped down her cheek. "I've ignored the street urchins back in New York. Taken a wide berth every time I see them. I've—"

His hand reached out to hers, and at the mere touch, all words vanished. An inconvenient truth rushed in. She had fallen in love with this most inappropriate but amazing man.

"Savannah, that is the work of the Holy Spirit. Jesus is calling you."

She shifted on the bench to face him. "Is it Jesus, or is it you? I've never felt anything like this before. When you're around..."

He lifted one hand to her face and thumbed the tear away. "I feel it too."

She caught his hand in hers to stop the insanity. "What are we going to do? Our worlds could not be further apart."

"We'll start with Jesus."

"Jesus—"

"Hear me out. There are two very different things colliding here. And I don't want one to blur the other. I agree that we have a...beautiful, effortless connection I can no longer deny. But there's something much more important."

"What? Speak plainly, Joseph. No riddles."

"You find the sermons and the Scripture readings like riddles. As it was in Jesus's time too. He spoke in stories and parables many didn't understand. But those who chose Him, and all who have said yes to the Holy Spirit down through the ages, have suddenly understood the Word of God. It will be the same for you."

"How do I say yes? I don't like this emptiness inside, this feeling that I somehow disappoint God. I'm sure it's what so many of us are feeling and why there is so much resistance to your words."

"You're right. And it only takes a mustard seed of faith to rectify that."

Savannah laughed. "Another parable, right?"

"Do you know how small a mustard seed is?"

"I don't think I do. I've not been in the kitchen much..." That truth was embarrassing to admit to a man who most likely knew far more about cooking than she did.

"A mustard seed is as small as or smaller than a grain of sand. Not much faith is needed to enter the kingdom of God. Do you want to feel at peace and live life with abundant purpose?" His eyes sparkled with life.

"Yes." She answered with assurance. She was so tired of the boredom and the lost, empty feeling inside her. And it had only intensified since she had found out her mother and father were not her biological parents. "Yes, I want that."

"I'll explain the process, and if you think you're ready, we'll pray together. It's simple, like ABC...A is for admitting that you're a sinner."

Savannah's eyebrows involuntarily raised. She had

never heard so blunt a statement. It did not feel good. Wasn't being a good person enough?

"Don't worry, Savannah. The Bible says in Romans 3:10 we're all sinners and fall short of the glory of God. You, me, everyone." He squeezed her hand.

She nodded. She was listening with her heart.

"The *B* is for believing in Jesus. Put your trust in Him for your salvation. John 3:16 says, 'For God so loved the world that He gave his only begotten Son, that whosoever believeth in Him should not perish, but have everlasting life.' Then you will become a child of God."

"Just like that? I become one of His children?"

"Yes. Just like that. John 1:12 says to all that receive Him, and believe in His name, He gives the right to become the children of God."

"And the *C*?"

"This can be the harder part. You must confess that Jesus is your Lord, first in prayer and then to others as the opportunity arises. Romans 10:9 puts it this way, 'If you confess with your mouth the Lord Jesus, and believe in your heart that God raised Him from the dead, you shall be saved.'" He paused. Kindness and joyful expectation flowed from his eyes. "Would you like to think about this decision?"

A pounding in Savannah's heart that had nothing to do with Joseph drew her. Her soul felt the squeeze of God's spirit. A different kind of love had beckoned since that first service. She wanted purpose. She longed for peace. She was ready. "I want to pray."

There on a bench, sitting beside the river, with birds flitting from tree to tree, chirping out a mingled melody, and the chatter of a nearby squirrel, Savannah gave her heart to Jesus. A peace like nothing she had ever experienced before spread through her, and all that had haunted her washed away.

"I feel so...so...light." Savannah snapped up from the bench and giggled like a schoolgirl.

"It's great, isn't it?" Joseph stood and smiled down at her.

Full-bodied laughter streamed from her lips, and she spun in a circle with her arms spread wide. "It's wonderful. So very wonderful."

She threw herself into Joseph's arms, and he hugged her tight. "Welcome to the family of God, Savannah. Welcome."

"Oh, my goodness. I can't wait to tell the others. My mother, my father—"

Joseph pulled out of her embrace.

A rustle in the bushes nearby gave Savannah a start. She slipped her arm into Joseph's. "What was that?"

"Probably just a river otter in the underbrush or a marsh rabbit. I've seen both."

Savannah relaxed her hold but didn't let go. They began walking back toward the clubhouse.

He halted their walk and looked her way. "Remember what I said about the hardest part...not all will consider your walk of faith a good thing. In fact, some may even resist—"

"Now, Joseph, wasn't it you who just told me a few minutes ago that the C stands for confess with my mouth? And quite frankly, I want everyone to experience this joy." She squeezed his arm. "I'm so happy I could burst."

Joseph chuckled and they began walking again. "I love the enthusiasm and I do understand. But not everyone will." He patted her hand that lay on his arm, then stopped just short of the main road and pulled free of her grasp.

Instant loss hit her.

"For your sake, we best not be seen together walking arm in arm." His jaw muscles knotted. "Especially without a chaperone. Not to mention our difference in social standings—and the other thing I mentioned that's colliding between us."

"But now I understand what you were saying. Social standing means nothing. We're all equal in the eyes of God. We all need a Savior—"

"You are absolutely right, but now you must learn to walk that fine line between not saying enough and saying too much. And steer clear of even the appearance of doing anything inappropriate."

"But—" A needle of concern stitched its way up her spine.

He pressed a finger to her lips "I would like nothing more than to have you on my arm, but we will not muddy the waters with trying to change the culture we live in overnight. We need to let the Holy Spirit guide."

His gaze felt different. Gentle and hopeful. That of a man to a woman. She could wait for him to realize what she already knew. God had made them for each other as surely as the waves pounded the eastern shoreline of Jekyll Island.

"I think I understand what you're saying. But I shall pray that God finds a way to bridge this gap. Weren't you just this morning telling the congregation that with God, nothing is impossible?"

His laughter boomed across the river, deepening the half-moon laugh lines on both sides of his mouth. "Listen to you, quoting Scripture."

She had a sudden urge to kiss those laughing lips... but then again, that would really muddy the waters.

CHAPTER 11

Savannah sat by the window in her suite, fully absorbed by the words upon the page. At a quick rap on the door of her bedroom, she glanced up from her Bible.

Emily poked her head in. "Your mother and father request your presence in their room before lunch."

"Thank you, Emily."

Emily's eyebrows lifted. "You don't have to thank me, miss. It's my job."

Over the last few days, Savannah's eyes had opened to those around her for the first time. In her previous world, the servants had moved about the resort doting on all the club members' whims almost invisibly in their drab gray uniforms. And each family brought along their personal lady's maid, as they had Emily, and gentleman's valet...all obscure until a few days ago when Savannah gave her heart to Jesus.

"But, Emily, I should thank you. You do so much for Mother and me. And I'm sorry I haven't paid much mind in the past."

A blush rose in Emily's cheeks as she dipped her head. The praise was clearly not something she was used to. An unfettered smile blossomed on her face, changing it from plain to beautiful. She slowly closed the door behind her.

How many things had Savannah missed that were now coming alive? Gratitude to those who served was just one of the mindful differences. She shut the Bible on her lap, so thankful that Joseph had given her one from the church to use. She had many questions to ask him.

She looked forward to an afternoon free of tea parties and social invites. The foursome were going for a bike ride. Savannah counted on the fact Walter and Elizabeth loved their time together. This allowed Joseph and her time to talk when she could learn of the vast mysteries the Scripture held. Verses now popped off the page, as though God was speaking directly to her. She could not get enough. But first, her parents... and lunch.

She gave a quick knock and entered her parents' room at the sound of Father's welcome. They sat around a small wicker table situated in the window alcove, and Father pointed to the spare chair. "Would you care for a cup of tea?"

"No, thank you. It will soon be lunch. Why did you

want to see me?"

Mother pursed her lips in disapproval and launched in. "Things have been brought to our attention that we're most concerned about."

Father patted Mother's hand. "If I may, Anna?"

She nodded at him, and he turned to Savannah. "My dear, word has gotten back to us that a few days ago...on Sunday, to be precise, you were seen down at the river in Reverend Bennett's arms."

Savannah had contemplated their curiosity at her reading the Bible and had prepared. But this? Surely, she would remember if she had been in Joseph's arms, for everything within her longed for that moment.

"We did meet down by the river—purely by accident, I might add—but I was not in his arms."

"This comes from a very reliable source," Mother said. Your Aunt Mary heard it directly from Yvonne Struthers. Apparently, she happened upon you."

Savannah did all she could to keep her tone kind. "Don't you see that your reliable source has gone from Yvonne, who has never cared for me, to Aunt Mary, then to you?"

"So there is no truth to this claim?"

Wait... In her joy after she prayed, she had indeed hugged Joseph. But she was not going to implicate him when he had been nothing but a gentleman. "No truth..."

The Holy Spirit instantly nudged her soul. *Tell the truth. You've been waiting for an opportunity to tell your parents about your newfound faith. Now is the time.*

"Well, to be honest, I did hug him, but it's not at all what you think."

Her mother shifted in her chair. Her back straightened. "So what, then?"

"I was hugging him because I was overjoyed with the gift he shared with me."

"What gift?" Father's eyes scanned her left hand, and his shoulders sagged in relief.

"I've been bursting with happiness and peace ever since, but I didn't know how to tell you."

Her parents shared a worried look between them and then pinned their focus back on her.

"Do tell," her mother instructed in a stern tone.

Savannah turned to her father. "Daddy, remember when I asked you if God was real?"

He nodded.

"Well, He is. The gift I received and was so overjoyed about is Jesus. I became a believer on Sunday, and I've never felt more at peace."

"What do you mean?" Her mother's voice went up an octave. "We all embrace some religion in our lives. After all, we do periodically attend the Episcopal Church. What is that one called, Henry?" She waved her hand at him.

"Trinity—"

"Yes, that's it. Trinity Church on Wall Street and Broadway."

"No, Mother, I don't mean attending an occasional mass here and there. I'm talking about a personal relationship with Jesus. A living, breathing experience that fills me up to overflowing. I don't know how to begin to describe how wonderful it is."

"Certainly, Jesus is not something to get worked up over, nor fanatical about." Mother shook her head in small, tight shakes.

Savannah could read the disappointment in her parents' eyes. Oh no...

"We forbid you to see any more of that man. He is taking this religion thing way too far, and you're falling into line with it." Her mother settled her teacup so hard in the saucer, a splash of tea stained the pristine white of the tablecloth.

"Mother, Joseph is living out his convictions, and now I shall live out mine."

"What exactly do you mean by that?" Father's voice rarely fluctuated in volume, but this time, it boomed.

Oh, dear Jesus, give me wisdom. Savannah had just read in the Bible about honoring her mother and father, so what should she do?

"It means that I will continue on this walk of faith wherever it leads." Savannah reached out and touched her father's hand. "Daddy, you know how lost and purposeless I have felt as of late. I shared my despondency and sadness with you. Remember?"

"Of course, I do, darling, but what has that got to do with this?"

"It's gone. One prayer and I'm at peace. There's a purpose to my life. How can it be wrong when I'm so powerfully transformed?" Yes, she was rambling, but she had to make them understand. "I'm happy, truly happy, for the first time in my life."

"This happiness has nothing to do with you and the reverend in each other's arms?" Her father looked directly at her, as if to read her mind.

"No. I swear, I was not in his arms in the way you think."

Mother frowned, the deep lines marring her still very beautiful face. "And there is nothing between you two in a romantic way?"

Savannah took a moment to think. Everything within her longed for a deeper relationship with Joseph, but their lives were worlds apart. It was as if God was telling her to trust Him with her feelings toward Joseph and concentrate on learning about her faith. But how to answer that question?

"I respect and like Joseph very much. He has become a good friend, but I'm aware, and so is he, how different our walks of life are."

Both her parents visibly relaxed into their chairs.

"I want to honor you as my parents and not sneak around to see Joseph behind your backs. I'm asking you to give me the little bit of time he has left here to enjoy our friendship, all under the watchful eyes of Walter and Elizabeth, of course." Savannah waited, holding her breath. She needed the time to learn all she could about God, but she dare not say too much about that at this point.

"Give us a few moments of privacy," Father said.

Savannah rose and walked from the room, shutting the door quietly behind her. Immediately, the argument began, and her mother's shrill voice rang out.

"No. That man cannot be allowed any more influence on our daughter."

Savannah's steps paused. Was she their daughter? That question kept roiling in her head, no matter how much she tried to stuff it down.

"Anna, if we push too hard, we'll lose. Savannah is a grown woman. She doesn't need our permission at twenty-two on who she can spend time with."

"But you know this so-called friendship could be dangerous. Didn't you see how her eyes lit up at the mention of his name?"

Savannah swallowed a knot lodged in her throat. Her raised heartbeat, the tremble of hands, or the way her insides tingled at the thought of Joseph were all indications of a greater reaction than friendship. It was no wonder her eyes gave away the truth.

"Can't say I noticed."

Mother huffed. "Men. You're all the same, clueless to the world around you."

"I am not clueless about the ramifications of pushing too hard." Father's voice boomed. "Look at what happened to the Dover family. They forbade their grown daughter to see that commoner, George, and the next thing they knew, she had run off and married him. The more restrictive we become, the more exciting it becomes. You know the old adage of forbidden fruit."

"Hmm, I do not like this." The *click, click, click* of Mother's heels signified her pacing back and forth.

"It's only two more weeks, and then she'll never see him again. He'll be on the mainland, and we'll be here until April. That should be plenty of time to cool both infatuations...with Joseph and with Jesus."

"You're right. I've seen this before, a spurt of religious zeal and then the bridge back to reality."

"Yes, my dear." Her father's voice softened. "As long as we don't burn that bridge in the process. All we need is a little time. And you know how worried we've been about her lately, yet now that hopelessness is gone. At least there's something positive about this situation."

"So we let her carry on seeing the man?"

"We can't stop it. And in a way, I'm glad she's distracted with this Jesus thing. She'll be less likely to succumb to the man's charms."

"Well, I can't say I feel comfortable with this decision. Lord only knows what our friends are going to think."

"Savannah is our focus. Not our friends."

Mother's voice softened. "You are right, my love. What would I do without you?"

87

The last thing Savannah heard as she walked away was her father's laughter.

She nibbled on her lower lip. How disappointed in her they would be when her love for Jesus did not diminish? For nothing in her life came close to the joy she felt inside, not even the presence of Joseph.

CHAPTER 12

Joseph drew a deep breath. This was the hardest thing the Holy Spirit had ever asked him to do. He stood with his bike in hand and prayed for strength as he awaited the arrival of Walter, Elizabeth, and Savannah.

Everything within Joseph longed to pursue a relationship with Savannah. He loved her spunk. Her intelligence. Her zest for adventure. And the attraction had only gotten stronger now that she was a child of God and they were no longer unequally yoked as the Good Book warned against. And yet the Father expected him to keep the focus on Savannah's relationship with Jesus, not on him...to spend their last two weeks together helping her grow in the Lord. He was not to be a distraction.

So much easier said than done.

Where were they? One glance at his pocketwatch told him he was still fifteen minutes early. With a swing of his leg, he was on his bike. He'd take one short ride around the compound.

His tour took him past millionaires' "cottages"—nothing short of mansions—with two to four chimneys, manicured grounds, and whimsical names like Hollybourne, Moss, and Mistletoe. His entire parsonage with its one central chimney back in New York City could be placed in one small corner—just another reminder of how disparate were his and Savannah's worlds. The servants' annex and black community's housing he whizzed past made reality even more sobering.

He rode back to the clubhouse, and there she stood, her golden hair shimmering in the sunlight. Everything about her exuded beauty.

Her hands tented over her eyes, shading them from the slant of the afternoon sun. At the sight of him, delight lit up her face, and her dark, luminous eyes rounded in laughter. "Ha. I beat you for once."

She looked so pleased with herself that he didn't have the heart to tell her he had been waiting. "Oh, you think so?"

"I know so."

The mischievous sparkle in her eyes almost undid him. All he wanted to do was drop his bike and gather her in his arms and never let go. "Have you seen Walter and Elizabeth?"

"They're coming. But I think the engaged couple are stealing a few minutes alone in the bike shed. If you get what I mean?"

Joseph laughed, but everything within him longed for the same uncomplicated love of being from the same social circles. A few weeks ago, he had no such pinings. Crazy what meeting the girl of his dreams could do.

"What?" Savannah cocked her head to one side.

Joseph looked away. He had been staring like a lovesick puppy. "What do you mean, *what*?"

"You're looking at me...all...I don't know...serious."

"I'm thinking about how far we've come from that first meeting. And how much I shall miss...everything on this island when it's time to leave." Now where had that come from? It was not the spiritual mentor tone he had hoped to set.

A wide grin split across her face. "Do you mean everything? Or do you mean me? Because you really don't strike me as the kind of man who is materialistic and pining for the lifestyle of the rich and famous."

"Must you be so blunt?"

Her laughter sounded like soft wind chimes. "Oh, you're one to talk. Have you heard one of your sermons?"

"Are they really that bad?"

"No, they're really that good. They led me to the Lord. And as for you missing me, because I know you will…" Her saucy grin turned serious. "I feel the same, Joseph. But I have faith that God will find a way…"

Her faith and optimism wafted from her like a sweet fragrance when he, the man of God, was not so sure.

Walter and Elizabeth arrived on their bikes. "Let's go. First one to the beach wins," Elizabeth challenged. Her curly auburn hair flew behind her as she cruised on by. Walter sped after her.

"Cheaters. You have a head start," Savannah yelled after them.

Joseph smiled. "Let them go. I'd rather take it slow and converse with you along the way. The time we have left is short, and I'm sure you have a thousand questions."

"There was a day I would never have let them win. Look what you've done to me." A bubble of laughter slipped free. "But I like your idea much better." She started pedaling. "My reading today was in John five, and I have a question…" Her voice faded away.

Spellbound, he snapped to it and followed her. They rode side by side, chatting all the way to the beach with question after question regarding what she had read. He was so proud of her, but he had a problem. He was falling more in love with her by the moment. Why couldn't his heart see what his head so clearly knew?

∽

*S*avannah awaited Emily's presence in her room to help her dress and do her hair for the afternoon Christmas tea at the Rockefellers'. Never had Savannah felt more in tune with the season. She had always resented that her parents preferred the warm, balmy temperatures of Jekyll Island over the possibility of snowflakes in New York. She rated her Christmases based on the arrival of white falling from the sky. This year it was different. The lack of snow didn't factor in. She was far more ready for Christmas than she had ever been, and it all had to do with her heart.

The only thing missing was a Christmas gift for Joseph. She'd planned ahead and bought gifts for her family back in New York but had no way of knowing the surprise that Jekyll Island had waiting for her.

There was no one she wanted to give a gift to more, but she had nothing to give. The island provided many recreational activities, but it didn't boast shopping.

A short rap on the door and Emily's head poked in. "Are you ready, my lady?"

Savannah waved her in. "You don't have to call me 'my lady,' as we've been together for as long as I remember. *Savannah* is just fine."

Emily's big blue eyes widened. She shook her slightly grayed head. "I could never do that, miss. That would be far too familiar."

"But...I insist."

"If your mother ever heard me addressing you in such a manner—"

"I love my mother dearly, but she's old-fashioned. Can we at least do it my way when we're alone?"

"As you wish." Emily didn't sound at all convinced. She moved about the room silently, throwing another log on the fire, then opening the doors of the ornate armoire.

How little Savannah knew about the middle-aged woman who had attended to her needs for years. And yet Emily had listened to her countless rants on the unbalanced rights of men versus women—but what about Emily's rights? What would it be like to be at the beck and call of someone all day? Shame filled Savannah's soul.

"I took the liberty of asking the chambermaid to take three of your dresses to laundry yesterday and have them freshly ironed. Which of these would you like?" Emily pointed to the three gowns imported from Paris.

Savannah took them in, then the dull gray dress with crisp white apron Emily wore day in and day out, and Savannah's stomach roiled. How privileged and spoiled she was just because of birthright. Or was it even birthright? Whose daughter was she? What if her birth mother was a woman like Emily?

"My lady...I mean, Savannah. Do you have a preference? The yellow one would look lovely with your dark eyes."

"Sure, Emily, that would be fine."

Emily set every layer of clothing out as she always did before starting Savannah's toilette, right down to the shoes and matching hat.

Savannah tried to think of some common ground, some way to make the conversation about Emily for a change. "You're so good at this, Emily. What would I do without you?"

"You would find many a lady's maid just waiting to step into my role. Now let me help you with your corset."

Is that how Emily saw it, that she was easily replaced? Was she fearful for her job? Savannah thought of her mother's somewhat austere ways and cringed. "But you're more to us than just a lady's maid. You're like family."

Emily's hands stalled for a moment from tightening the corset. "That is kind of you to say, Miss Savannah."

"I mean that with all my heart."

Emily looked into the mirror in front of Savannah and gave a rare smile. She continued with her work of dressing Savannah. The corset cover, the bustle, then the dress—each layer added further suffocation akin to the trappings of Savannah's affluent life.

"There now, my lady...I mean, Miss Savannah. You look as pretty as a picture. Come, we have only your hair to do." She pointed to the chair in front of the dressing table. "You have an afternoon tea at the Rockefellers', so how about something a little more elaborate. Perhaps the Edwardian twist?"

"That would be lovely. Thank you."

Emily lifted a few locks of Savannah's hair in one hand and the brush in the other. "Your hair is so thick and beautiful all swept up in that style."

Again, Emily had skillfully turned the conversation back to Savannah, so she prayed. *Lord, give me the wisdom to find a way to reach into Emily's life in a meaningful way. Help me exude love so she sees a change that points to You. Show me Your ways, Oh Lord, so that others will be drawn to You.*

Savannah caught Emily's eye in the mirror. "You've been with us for as long as I can remember."

"Yes. Since before you were born."

"You never talk of your family, your life, your hopes and dreams, yet you let me chatter on constantly. I'd like to get to know you."

"That would be inappropriate, Miss Savannah. Servants are to be seen, not heard. Your mother has taught you that over the years, and I'm sure she—"

"I'm not talking about my mother. I'm referring to you and me at times like this when we're alone. You know most everything there is to know about me, and I know virtually nothing about you. I would like a friendship that goes both ways."

"Friendship?" A distressed look soaked into Emily's eyes, and her fingers trembled slightly as they pinned Savannah's hair into place.

"Yes. How about we start with where you were born and lived as a child?"

"No." Emily's voice was sharp. "Your mother would not be pleased. We must keep things as they are."

Savannah's shoulders sagged. How was she to be a witness for Jesus when the walls that society had built were too high to climb? Emily seemed indisputably closed, even frightened, to bridge the gap. Savannah would have to talk to her mother. Maybe if she relaxed a bit, Emily would follow suit. After all, such elitism was quite old-fashioned. The world was changing, and it was time they changed with it.

"Are you all ready for Christmas? Less than a week to go." Emily's voice had softened, and Savannah could tell she was trying hard to smooth out what had just happened.

"All except one detail."

"And what is that?" Emily picked up another pin and put it into place.

"Well, you know how I told you about my new friendship with Joseph? I'd like to get him a gift, but there's nothing on the island."

"I have an idea." Friendliness was back in Emily's voice. "The superintendent, Mr. Grob, told the staff that tomorrow Captain Clark is making a run into Brunswick on the *Jekyll Island* steamer for all last-minute shoppers. Your mother has already booked me to run an errand for her. Why don't you join me for the afternoon?"

"Why, that's a perfect plan. Mother will not object if you're with me, and I would love to get Joseph something. But I won't bother sharing that part with Mother. She wouldn't understand."

"You like that young man, don't you?"

Heat rushed to Savannah's cheeks. She glanced into the mirror. There was no hiding the truth. "I do. He's become a good friend. My head knows there is a huge gap in our social standing, but there's no telling my heart that fact."

Emily squeezed her shoulders and leaned close to her ear. "Love has a way of sneaking up on one, doesn't it?"

Savannah swiveled in her chair. "Why, Emily, are you going against your better judgement and alluding to something personal from your past?" she asked with a tease in her voice. "Because that sounds as though you speak from experience."

"I can tell you this much. It was many years ago..." Her blue eyes grew noticeably softer. "...but I shall never forget."

"Oh, please tell me more."

Emily swiveled the chair back toward the mirror and fiddled with last touches. "We were so in love, but Mama and Papa insisted my sister and I get on the boat to America with them. Johnny swore he would come the following year. He scrimped and saved enough to get on a less-than-reputable vessel that had an outbreak of typhoid. He died en route. It was the one time I wished I had disobeyed my parents and stayed in England with the man I loved."

Savannah stood and drew Emily into a quick embrace. "Thank you for trusting me...but what a sad story."

Emily pulled out of the hug. "There now, my lady, you're ready for the day. If you'll excuse me, I must attend to your mother." She slipped out of the door, but not before Savannah caught the tears in her eyes.

CHAPTER 13

Savannah stepped onto the *Jekyll Island* steamer. A crisp breeze whipped a few strands of her upswept hair free of its pins. She pulled her shawl tighter around her shoulders. It was a tad cooler than she would've preferred for a boat trip, but the cerulean-blue sky stretching above beckoned her to the sides of the rail rather than the warmth of the inside.

The pungent mixture of marshland, fish, and sea salt filled her senses. Savannah drew in a deep breath. There was something about that smell that beckoned her to worlds beyond the borders of what she knew.

The boat slowly reversed from the dock and slipped into the deeper murky waters of the Jekyll River. They were off, and Savannah had high hopes for the afternoon. She was on a mission to find that one perfect gift that suited the man she had come to know. She had no idea what it would be but was confident it would present itself.

"Do you mind if I slip inside, my lady?" Emily asked. "These older bones are rather on the chilly side."

"Of course. I'm not sure how long I'll last out here, but I love the wind on my face." Savannah turned her attention to the banks of the river as she looked for wildlife.

"What are you doing here?" The rich timber of Joseph's voice startled her.

Savannah turned with an instant smile to the man beside her. "I guess I could ask you the same." A weakness in the hollow of her knees made her grip the rail with renewed vigor.

"This is a welcome treat. Me, you, and the Marshes of Glynn." His dimples danced.

A flush of heat worked up from her neck to her face. "We are not quite to the marsh land yet, but I'm looking for wildlife." She ripped her gaze from his and scanned the riverbank to find her equilibrium.

"There." Joseph pointed. "A blue heron."

Savannah followed the direction of his strong arm. The bird high-stepped through the shallow waters with its yellow beak pointed down.

"It's stalking its next meal."

Savannah giggled. "Stalking. That's a weird choice of words. Is that what you're doing to me?"

"Ha. I could ask the same of you. When did you arrange to make this trip?"

Savannah didn't care to answer him and give away her secret.

"Uh-ha, I can tell by that little grin of yours that your plans are most recent. I scheduled this with Captain Clark over a week ago."

"Fine, then. But I assure you, I have no need to stalk any man." She turned her head to the water with a decided jerk.

His laugh echoed across the water. "No, I don't suppose you do, pretty lady."

Quiet descended between them as the boat sliced through the calm waters of the tidal creek. The Marshes of Glynn spread out for miles on both sides. The cordgrass swayed in the breeze like a golden sea of wheat.

"Sidney Lanier wrote a beautiful poem about this very place called *The Marshes of Glynn*. Have you ever read it?" Joseph asked.

"No. I don't believe I have."

"Oh, it's a must. When my father asked me if I would agree to preach on this island, I started to do some reading about its history, and the club. I ran across the poem. I tend to remember random bits and pieces...

"Free

By a world of marsh that borders a world of sea.

Sinuous southward and sinuous northward the shimmering band

Of the sand-beach fastens the fringe of the marsh to the folds of the land.

Inward and outward to northward and southward the beach-lines linger and curl,
As a silver-wrought garment that clings to and follows the firm sweet limbs of a girl..."

"Why Joseph, that is amazingly romantic—the fact you can remember and so eloquently bequeath the gift of poetry." Savannah clapped as though she was at the theatre.

"Would you care for a few more lines, my lady?"

"I would." Savannah was mesmerized. The cut of his tall, lean frame, his strong profile gazing out at the marsh, the low bass of his voice with perfect inflection, and the gift of such an intelligent mind.

"*Oh, what is abroad in the marsh and the terminal sea?*
Somehow my soul seems suddenly free,
From the weighing of fate and the sad discussion of sin
By the lengths and the breadth and the sweep of the marshes of Glynn.
God out of knowledge and good out of infinite pain
And sight out of blindness and purity out of a stain.
As the marsh hen secretly builds on the watery sod,
Behold I will build me a nest on the greatness of God:
I will fly in the greatness of God as the marsh hen flies,
In the freedom that fills all the space 'twixt the marsh and the skies."

Savannah could barely speak. She swallowed a lump in her throat. "That was beautiful, but no small piece as you so humbly claimed." She could've stood there and listened to him for hours. She longed for his voice to carry on...and on...for their life to carry on together, where she could learn more of the mysteries this man had to offer.

"I know." He turned to her. The smoky gray of his eyes deepened, glowing warmly. "In truth, I can remember most every word of that nine-hundred-and-ninety-seven-word poem."

"You are the most fascinating man I've ever met. But how do you know how many words are in the poem, much less memorize them?"

"A lot more rattles around up here than I let on." He smiled and pointed to his head. "Only a select few know my story."

"Will you tell me?" Savannah longed to know everything about him, but would he open up to her?

"People stereotype a man who has chosen the life I have. But God gave me a bright mind, and I was a gifted learner from a child up. I was given a scholarship to Columbia and disappointed many of my teachers, as well as my father, when I chose to be a preacher."

"But I thought you told me your father is a preacher?"

"He is. But that was not the life he wanted for his son. My father somewhere along the road got caught up in pleasing others, but that's a whole other story for another day. His only goal now is to see me become the most popular reverend in New York, and beyond. You could say he lives vicariously through me. I fear I will greatly disappoint him. This trip to Jekyll Island was all about rubbing shoulders with the who's who, and all I've succeeded in doing is poke and prod. I will come away from this island far from popular and likely shunned from ever returning. But I followed the Lord's lead and met..."

He turned from the water to look directly at Savannah. Her heart pumped in erratic fashion at his loving gaze.

"...the most amazing woman." He lightly stroked the curve of her cheek before dropping his hand.

With a sharp intake, she held her breath. Would he declare his love?

"A woman I would love to spend the rest of my life with, but it can never be."

"Joseph, I long for the same—"

He shook his head and grasped her hand. A shot of awareness spread up her arm. "Please don't say more, as it will only make the leaving that much harder. We have Christmas in a few short days. I have a commitment to fulfill, and then I shall be gone. Me to my world, and you to yours."

"But, Joseph, surely, you believe as you just quoted... 'I will fly in the greatness of God as the marsh hen flies. In the freedom that fills all the space 'twixt the marsh and the skies.'"

"Walk with me. We're receiving attention, and I don't want to compromise your reputation. But I need a few moments of privacy to help you understand what I'm saying without others watching us through the windows or overhearing our conversation." He pulled her along the side of the boat to a private alcove where only sea and sky could record the moment.

"I don't think I want to understand." Savannah's stomach lurched. Joseph's expression looked serious.

"You ask me what I believe...and I've prayed and pondered and agonized, in fact. What is best for you, my dear Savannah, is to not encourage whatever is happening between us. You'll find a man in your world who will bring you happiness and ensure things are in keeping with that to which you've become accustomed."

"No. I don't agree." Her heart wrenched as if he'd grabbed it and ripped it from her body.

"Please, Savannah..."

She'd had enough of words. Words that sliced her heart in two.

"Don't make this harder than—"

She yanked the lapel of his coat close and pressed her mouth against his.

He drank like a man receiving a drink in the heat of the desert that only she could provide. He crushed her closer, their lips speaking what words could not. They kissed long and lingering, savoring each other. He would pull back and then drop his lips to hers again. From gentle to passionate, their lips, their hearts, their souls sang the same song.

"Come with me, young lady." Emily's stern voice cut in, and they jumped apart. "You're entrusted into my care, and your parents would not be pleased." She locked her arm into Savannah's and glared at Joseph. "As for you...a man of the cloth, leading a young, vulnerable woman astray...well, you should be ashamed of yourself."

CHAPTER 14

After Savannah's maid had pulled her into the cabin of the steamer, Joseph stood in the alcove without moving. The boat sliced its way into the open waters of the Brunswick River that fed into the Atlantic. The rough ocean pushed against the bow of the boat as fiercely as the attraction to Savannah pressed against his heart. But the steamer held its course where he had failed.

The second Savannah had placed her lips on his, he was a goner. He could have pulled back...should have pulled back. But instead, he enjoyed every moment. Even initiated more. And her maid was right—his behaviour had been inexcusable, especially when he knew he couldn't follow his heart and propose marriage. He had put her reputation in question, all because of a selfish desire to have a memory to cherish in the years to come. He had not been prepared for the most amazing kiss of his life, or his unfettered reaction.

Oh God. What have I done? And what would You have me do?

Silence.

Why did he hear nothing when he most needed wisdom, yet other times received messages he did not care to preach? Such as those he had delivered on Jekyll Island. He could not put God in a box any more than he could fly *"twixt the marsh and the skies.*

Well, he'd face whatever repercussions came from this and take full responsibility. But that kiss had been worth the stolen moment, and he would never be sorry. It would be his only solace for many lonely months to come.

~

Savannah walked the streets of Brunswick with Emily. Their time was almost gone, and still she had not found anything befitting for Joseph. If it came to having to let him go, she wanted something he would remember her by.

Please God, You know how I feel. There are no secrets between us. You created in me this heart that beats faster and these eyes that see the extraordinary in Joseph, and this mind that refuses to forget how special we are together. That kiss only enhanced the certainty. Surely, God, You know what gift Joseph could use. The prayer no sooner slipped into the heavens than a jewelry store across the street caught her attention.

"We must get back soon." Emily was looking at her timepiece, and everything fell into place for Savannah. Emily had barely spoken to her since that incident on the boat. Her quiet countenance, pouty visage, and furrowed brow spoke volumes. Savannah had betrayed her trust.

"One more stop across the street."

"You have exactly ten minutes, and when I say it's time to go, it's time to go." Her voice was stern and unyielding. "The last thing I want on my conscience is not getting you back to your parents for Christmas."

"Agreed." Savannah hurried across the street.

Bells jingled from above the door as she entered.

"Good afternoon. How may I help you?" A short, rounded man with a head as shiny as a coffee bean smiled at her. His perfectly appointed suit, which hid his bulges to best advantage, spoke of quality.

"I'm looking for a pocket watch but must catch the boat back to Jekyll Island in less than ten minutes."

His eyes lit up at the words *Jekyll Island*. "I have just the one for you."

He pulled out an item from the top shelf of a glass display case and wasted not a second in the description. "Notice all the features...porcelain dial, eighteen-karat gold case, fine rounded corners polished with a decorative pattern on the flat surface." He lovingly turned the watch in his perfectly manicured hands. "Look at the stunning detail." He held it just out of her reach, obviously not prepared to take the risk of her not being a legitimate buyer or even her snatching the watch and making a run for the door.

Savannah suppressed a smile. "It's lovely."

"It boasts only the best inner workings...ruby jewels in gold settings, set in nickel plates. This piece is of the finest quality, handmade in Switzerland with precision craftsmanship. You won't find a more handsome pocket watch anywhere."

"The price?" Savannah asked sweetly with her best smile.

He quoted an outrageous amount, but Savannah did not blink. "I'm sure you are a hard-working proprietor and do not need me haggling the price. Can you wrap it up in..." She turned to Emily, whose rounded mouth closed slowly. "How much time do I have?"

Emily regained composure and looked at the time piece hanging around her neck. "Exactly four minutes."

Savannah faced the proprietor. "Can you wrap it up in four minutes?"

The man tried to hold back his smile and keep things professional, but he was clearly pleased. "I most certainly can, miss."

Savannah opened her reticule and counted out the money. Good thing she had been far too bored as of late to shop. She had not spent a penny of her allotted allowance in the past few months and had cash to spare.

Joseph would have this gift for years to come, as a reminder of her undying love. And maybe God would yet grant a miracle and they would reminisce each year —of the day of their first kiss back in the Christmas of 1906.

～

"I must talk to you about what happened earlier before we get back." Emily slid into a seat beside Savannah.

They were in a private corner of the inside of the boat, but Savannah spoke in a low voice. "Are you planning on telling Mother and Father?"

"I must." Emily fiddled with a handkerchief in her hand, folding and unfolding it.

"Why? I need this next week with him, and then I'll tell Mother and Father myself. If you say anything now, Christmas will be ruined, and our last bit of time together will be denied. I love him, Emily, and I'm sure he loves me. And I plan to find a way to—"

"Has he said those words...that he loves you?"

"Well, not exactly. We have both been keeping a safe distance, but after that kiss today, I know."

"You're far too naïve, just like..." Emily's voice trembled.

"Like who?"

"Never you mind. Just take my word for it." Her

words came out harsh and unyielding. "It will never work."

Emily had always been soft spoken and kind to Savannah, but twice in a matter of days, she had barked out a response. "Emily, why are you so upset? I know I wasn't supposed to be alone with Joseph, but a kiss is not a crime between two people who really care for each other."

"A kiss today, and a whole lot more tomorrow."

"Joseph is not like that. He would never dishonor God in that way, and neither would I."

"I best tell you a story...how I know that the different classes will never work." Emily turned toward Savannah and took both of her hands, giving a light squeeze before letting go. "I care deeply for you. I've been with your family since before you were born, and I don't want what happened to my sister to happen to you..."

"Your sister?"

Emily nodded. "Both of us were hired at the same time by your mother and father. I, to be trained to be your mother's lady's maid as her maid was retiring, and my sister was to work in the kitchen. She had such a love for cooking and rose quickly within the kitchen staff to be the right-hand assistant to the chef."

"What is your sister's name?"

"Her name was Isabel."

"Was?"

Shadows fell across Emily's eyes. "Yes, was. She is no longer with us."

"Oh, Emily, I'm sorry." Savannah reached out to touch Emily's hand, but she pulled it free.

"It was a long time ago, and the pain is not as severe as it was...but this story is still hard to tell, so best not to—"

"I won't interrupt again," Savannah assured her.

Emily nodded but looked down at her lap. Her hands squeezed so tightly together that her knuckles were turning white. She took a moment to continue.

"A handsome, wealthy man, whom I will not name, came to visit your parents and raved about the dinner that was served. It so happened that evening that the chef had been sick, and my sister had been the one to step into the head role.

"The man insisted he meet the cook, and Isabel was brought up from the kitchen. My sister was a comely girl, with beautiful blond hair, big brown eyes that drew attention, and well...very attractive in every way.

"This man began pestering your father. He wanted to hire Isabel as his head chef, and Isabel wanted the opportunity. Over the course of a few months, your father and mother finally relented. I was not happy. She was my younger sister, and I was very protective of her, but it was what Isabel wanted. After she left the Ensworth household, I didn't get to see her much. Just a few Sunday afternoons here and there. She was always busy and always making excuses every time I sent a message to her. Then one Sunday, we met after months apart, and she was decidedly pregnant."

Savannah gasped.

"The wealthy man who had offered her the job as the head chef obviously had other plans. The transition to head chef never happened. Instead, he made my sister believe he loved her, and maybe he did, but an aristocrat is never going to do right by a servant girl.

He tucked her away in an apartment...away from the eyes of society and his household. She believed he would marry her. I did not. For their worlds were too different. What would she know about being a lady, entertaining his guests, intermingling with other women of that social standing? She was a poor servant girl who knew nothing of how to dress, how to speak, how to parade about as the privileged upper class, the elite of society. Just as your Joseph would be lost in your world."

"But Joseph has an education. He is very intelligent and—"

"So was my sister. She had a bright mind. How do you think she picked up on how to cook as well as a head chef with no formal training? No. You must face the fact, Joseph will never be accepted, never fit in. He has no status, no wealth, no family bloodlines."

"What happened to your sister?" Savannah's voice trembled as she tried to change the way the conversation was going. She didn't want to see the parallel between the stories.

"The man of aristocratic birth and very old money could not find the strength to do right by her. He married another woman of his class when Isabel was eight months pregnant. I think he intended to keep both his wife and mistress, but Isabel landed up on our doorstep in labor. The stress had brought on the baby a few weeks early."

"Oh, my goodness." Savannah's hand flew to her mouth.

"Your mother, God bless her kindness, took Isabel in, and she had her baby in the very house you have grown up in. Isabel had difficulty birthing the baby. That coupled with a broken heart and no will to live resulted in her death."

"Oh, Emily." Savannah touched Emily's arm gently.

"I stir up this old story, though it pains me greatly, to warn you. Even if you think you love Joseph, or he loves you…your worlds are too different. Do your heart a big favor and let him go back to his life, and you carry on with yours."

"But Emily—"

"No *buts*. Can you honestly see yourself as a preacher's wife attending to the needs of others? Because that's what a preacher's wife does. Not to mention, living in a small house where you would have to do the cooking, cleaning, and washing of your own clothes. You would not have help getting dressed, or someone coming into your room in the morning and starting your fire to get your room toasty warm before you step out of bed."

Savannah hadn't thought of the possibility of not having money. "You think my parents would disown me, and I would have no funds?"

"Yes. I think they would oppose it so strongly that this would be one of the conditions."

"But what if Joseph joined my life?"

Emily had the nerve to laugh. "I sat in on his sermons these past few weeks. That man is nothing if he is not sincerely opposed to the frivolous lives of the wealthy and privileged. And he is a gifted and passionate preacher. You would take that from him?"

"I...hadn't thought that far ahead."

"Well, you need to. For his sake as well as your own." Emily stood. "You need to end whatever is going on between you. Now, if you'll excuse me, I need a breath of fresh air."

"Emily? One more question."

The maid turned toward her.

"What happened to the baby your sister had. Did it die too?"

Emily's shoulders sagged and wilted around her trim frame. "The baby didn't die, but I was not able to care for her. My father had since passed, and the little bit I was making had to go to support my ailing mother. I couldn't compromise my job." Sadness laced her voice. "She was adopted into a good family."

"Do you ever get to see your niece?"

A troubled light stole into Emily's eyes. "The details of adoptions are not public information. Now, please excuse me, miss." She turned and marched off with a briskness in her step.

Savannah took a deep breath. Could she be that child? How ironic, for that would make Joseph's station in life higher than hers. Yet what did it matter? She'd been raised the only child and heir of a powerful banking tycoon.

CHAPTER 15

Savannah's head ached from all the thinking. She'd barely slept the night before and had yet to venture out of her room the next morning. She sank onto the chair by the window and sat with her hands pressed against the pounding behind both temples.

Everything within her longed to draw Joseph closer. Not for the reasons she had in the beginning—to win a challenge and have him succumb to her charms. But because she had truly fallen in love with him.

However, everything Emily stated was true. She was no preacher's wife, and she certainly didn't know how to take care of herself. The more she thought about how all her basic needs were met, the more insecure she became. What could she do with excellence? Play tennis, play the piano, play the perfect hostess...everything was a form of play.

And she would never want to lead Joseph from the work of the Lord. He would be miserable. Her only choice was to savor this last bit of time...Christmas through New Year's, and then let him go. It took some real pleading on Savannah's part to get Emily to agree not to involve her parents while Joseph was on the island. Savannah had to shamelessly tug on Emily's heart strings about the pain of lost love and promise to have an honest conversation with her parents the minute Joseph left.

A tap on her bedroom door broke into her brooding. "Come in."

Elizabeth poked her head in. "How was your trip into Brunswick yesterday?"

Savannah waved her in. "Oh, Elizabeth. What have I done?"

Elizabeth settled on the bed across from her, and the story poured out.

Her friend heaved a sigh. "You've both done exactly what I feared. I see the way he looks at you and can tell he loves you as much as you love him."

"He hasn't voiced that."

Elizabeth raised one brow. "He doesn't need to. His eyes tell the story. In the ways that count, you two make the perfect couple. There's a connection between you that's undeniable. A sense of humor and hankering for adventure. A penchant for discussing the deep things, such as God, politics, social injustices, even your women's suffrage group—all the things you've longed for a man to understand and support. But..."

"Yes. I know there is a very big *but*."

"It's Christmas in a few short days, and you have one more week to figure it out. Surely, you and that great big God of yours can come up with something. Doesn't the Bible instruct not to worry?"

Savannah laughed, though the tears lay just beneath the surface. "You're right. I need to snap out of this and enjoy the time we've been given."

"I know just the thing." Elizabeth jumped up from the bed. "I'm going to keep you busy. All the young people are going down to the beach for a bonfire tonight after the children's Christmas program, and you're coming."

"Ahh, I don't know—"

"Well, I do and that's settled. Mr. Grob said the local women are decorating the church this afternoon. Why don't we volunteer to help, as you're all about a good cause these days?"

"Christmas program? I wonder why Joseph didn't mention anything about it to me."

"Because Mr. Grob organizes this special Christmas party for the employees' children. Apparently, names are given to all the members who are here during the season to donate enough to get each child a new outfit and a toy for Christmas, and we're expected to attend in support of the families."

"Hmm, I've been to this program other years, and it

must be one of those charitable things Daddy says they contribute to. Funny they've never mentioned it."

"Maybe they don't want to brag about what they give. Now come on. The decorating will get you out of this room and your mind off the obvious." She pulled at Savannah's hand.

"All right. All right. I'm coming. But how will it get my mind off the obvious when I'll come face to face with Joseph?"

"Face the giant and it shall fall—so says the story of David and Goliath."

Savannah linked her arm into her friend's as they walked out of the bedroom and down the hall. "Well, aren't you the little Bible scholar?"

Elizabeth laughed. "Nope. No scholar, but I do know enough of the basics to challenge you."

"And look where your initial challenge got me."

Elizabeth's expressive green eyes widened. "I'm truly sorry, Savannah."

"Don't you worry." She patted Elizabeth's arm. "Because of you and your challenge, I came to church, and I met the love of my life...well, actually two loves." They stepped down off the veranda into the sun. "Jesus and Joseph."

The fresh air on the walk to the church cleared Savannah's headache, and the lemony glow and warmth of sunshine on her shoulders buoyed her spirits. She had no idea how God was going to solve the dilemma of her heart. All she knew was that she was no longer alone, and He would give her strength.

By the time she lifted the hem of her skirt to take the steps into Faith Chapel, hope had risen. Joseph was nowhere in sight, but when they offered to help, the two black women welcomed them in.

Ophelia doled out the jobs, and Aleathia knew the best ways to decorate with local ferns, boughs, and flowers. Their banter back and forth was like that of old friends.

Savannah tied pinecones and pine boughs together and hung them with a large silver bow at the end of each pew. The woodsy scent filled her senses with renewed joy. Christmas was the season of miracles, and she needed one.

An inspired thought came to mind. If she learned the basics of cleaning, cooking, and caring for herself, Joseph could not object to her joining his life. Her heavy heart lifted. She aimed to tell him that plan if she could only get him alone.

Elizabeth laid out pine boughs along the front of the sanctuary. She interspersed the arrangement with red velvet bows and gold bells hanging down.

Savannah surveyed the chapel with pride. It was amazing what four industrious women could do and the sense of accomplishment she found in working with her hands.

When Mr. Grob and Joseph came in lugging a large fir tree, it took all Savannah's self-control not to stare.

She hadn't talked to Joseph since that fateful kiss. At her smile, he almost dropped his end of the tree.

"Hang onto it, Joseph. I know how distracting a pretty girl can be." Mr. Grob's voice held a tease. "This tree came all the way from New York, and the members paid good money for it. They wouldn't be impressed if it was less than perfect."

Joseph's face colored, and Savannah turned back to her work. She stifled the joy that bubbled inside. That one look proved he cared for her as much as she did for him.

Ophelia waved the two men over to the corner that she had cleared, and Mr. Grob worked at getting the tree in the stand.

Joseph slipped out but returned carrying a box. "Okay, ladies, the fun part. Here are the decorations."

"If it's so fun, why don't you join us?" Aleathia's wide, toothy grin split across her deep-chocolate face.

"You didn't think I would leave now, did you?"

"Why, Reverend Bennett, you are indeed a preacher full of surprises." Ophelia's almond-shaped eyes teased in merriment. "Or is it a special someone who has you lingering?"

Mr. Grob's hearty laugh echoed through the chapel. "Well said, Ophelia."

Did everyone know? Savannah's cheeks burned hot. Here she thought they had been so discreet. Did their love literally sing from their veins?

Savannah dipped her fingers into the box the same

time as Joseph, and their hands touched. A shot of awareness scuttled up her arm.

He pulled his hand free as if he had placed it in a flame.

If even the staff could see what was happening between them, it was time to face the dilemma together.

"Are you going to the bonfire tonight on the beach?" Savannah whispered.

He looked at her with sadness in his eyes. "I...I'm not sure."

"Why aren't you sure?"

"It's Sunday tomorrow, and I need to prepare for the sermon." He glanced away.

A heavy knot settled in Savannah's stomach. She knew from previous conversations he had his sermons mapped out before he even arrived on the island. He was avoiding her. Like the flowing Jekyll river in a storm, the troubled waters of her soul rippled with concern.

CHAPTER 16

Savannah woke up early Christmas morning. The joy of the season bubbled up inside in a way she had never experienced before. Joseph was clearly avoiding her, but a hope that only God could give stirred within.

Though she'd prayed to have her feelings for Joseph eradicated, every moment in his presence heightened the love. There was no going back. God's will included all that was happening.

She slipped from her bed and padded across the room to the window. With a peek between the curtains, the certainty of a gloomy day lay before her. Steady rain poured down. A bone-deep chill shivered through her body. She headed to the hearth, where a few embers remained. If she rang the bell, Emily would come running, but she'd watched the chambermaids build and start the fire the night before. She could do this.

After she carefully arranged the smaller kindling at the bottom and a few larger pieces on top, smoke billowed, but there was no flame.

If only she could surprise Emily with this one small success in taking care of herself. She'd already persuaded Emily to teach her the basics of doing her own hair, but the next part of her plan would ask a lot more support from the maid. Savannah needed to impress her. That fire had to burn.

Her writing paper sat on the small table by the window, and she smiled. With a scoot across the room, she grabbed some pages, crumpled them up, and headed back to the hearth. She poked them close to the smoking embers, then picked up the bellow that sat on the hearth. With a gust of air, the fire burst into flame.

Savannah giggled and jumped up and down like a child. She pulled up a chair and sat with her Bible in front of the heat. What a great start to Christmas day. She had high hopes that she would find a private moment with Joseph. A glance across the room to where his Christmas present sat boxed up pretty with a bow brought a smile to her lips.

Emily's slight rap on the door was distinguishable. She entered without acknowledgement. Her blue eyes popped open wide. "Well, look at you, sitting beside a fire that you alone built." There was pride in her voice.

"I plan to learn a whole lot more," Savannah admitted. "If I'm ever to join Joseph in his life, I need to be prepared."

Emily's eyebrows tugged together. As if frozen in a weightiness of indecision, she stopped short. "Child, you must give up this fanciful dreaming of yours. You're the daughter of a proud man, and he would never allow such a thing. And your mother would have a conniption if she heard but a whisper of this."

"Am I?"

"Are you what?"

"The daughter of Henry and Anna Ensworth?"

Emily's eyebrows shot up , and her mouth opened and closed, but nothing came out.

Savannah had not meant to speak the words, but they had spilled out. Emily's reaction confirmed the truth.

The maid found her voice. "Why ever would you ask such a thing?" Her words came out strangled. She avoided eye contact and hurried across the room to make the bed.

"To be honest with you, I overheard my parents talking. I know I'm adopted."

"Then why ask me? You should talk to them. However, I'd strongly recommend leaving things as they are." Emily's voice wavered. Her hands trembled as she fluffed the pillows.

Why was she doing the work of the chambermaid if not to avoid the truth? Savannah went to the other side of the bed and joined in the task. She needed Emily on her side. "I've felt as if I'm adrift at sea for a long time. I don't like this life of leisure, and that's why I've fought for the same rights as a man. To work, to have purpose, to be part of something bigger than myself."

Emily plunked down a pillow. "That comes with marriage and babies, and getting involved in charities—"

"No. Now I know there's more."

"This is not a discussion I can have with you." She stopped fussing with the bed and planted both hands on her hips. "And I'd appreciate you refraining from confiding in me any further. I don't want to be dishonest with your mother when she catches wind of all of this."

"But, surely, you understand."

"It matters not what I understand or think. I'm not your mother, and I will speak of this no more." She pursed her lips tightly together.

Savannah had hoped Emily would aid in the process of her learning how to cook, clean, and manage a household. But that was not to be. Oh well. Savannah caught onto things easily. She'd figure this out with or without Emily's help.

～

Savannah entered her parents' suite and placed a kiss on Daddy's and Mother's cheeks. "Merry Christmas."

"And to you, my darling girl," Daddy replied.

As usual, far too many gifts for three people encircled the small tree in the corner of the room. What extravagance, when the island children were thrilled with one toy and new outfit, and worse yet, others were staving off cold and hunger in the streets of New York City.

Savannah settled in a chair near the glowing fire, and the exchanging of gifts began. But she was anything but settled. Her unplanned conversation with Emily about her parentage brought the subject to the surface, and it took every bit of strength she had to stuff it down. Today was not the day to create drama.

"Oh Savannah, this is absolutely lovely." Mother lifted an elaborate hat with a double row of ribbons, roses of different hues, and a peacock plume from the new handcrafted hatbox.

"Thought you might like that."

"Oh, but I do."

Savannah opened up box after box of custom-made dresses, hats, parasols, gloves, and boots. None of it would be suitable for the new life she hoped to embark upon in 1907. She finally opened a present with a simple blouse and skirt and squealed out her delight.

"You now get excited?" Her mother's expression was aghast.

"It's just what I need."

"Need for what, my dear?" Her father looked up in surprise.

Savannah could've lied and said the expected—bicycling or traveling, but she spoke the truth. "This clothing will better suit my future. They're perfect."

Daddy's bushy brows furrowed together. "Wouldn't the other presents be a better fit for your social calendar?"

"Yes. What exactly do you mean by that remark?" Mother gave Savannah her utmost attention.

What could Savannah say? She'd allowed her dreams to spill out, but Joseph had promised her nothing. She might not have any future with him. And he certainly didn't know the lengths she was willing to go to in order to fit into his life. In fact, he'd ignored her since that kiss on the boat.

"Oh, it's nothing." Savannah waved her hand. She could minimize the situation, but she couldn't blatantly lie.

"What aren't you telling us?" Father was not to be fooled.

"Indeed. You've been most secretive since this religious conversion of yours." Her mother waved her new fan in front of her face. It always turned flushed when she was agitated. "You'd think that Jesus would improve your life, not make you dishonest."

"I'm not being dishonest." Savannah was caught between her dreams and her current reality. Should she tell them?

Mother lifted her chin. "Withholding information is a form of deceit."

"You and Daddy are hardly ones to judge on that account." Savannah bit out her reply.

"Just what do you mean?" Daddy leaned forward in his chair.

"I know I'm adopted."

"You most certainly are not." Mother's brows rose.

"Yes, Mother, I am. I overheard you and Daddy talking."

"I...we...ahh." Mother's body crumpled in the chair. Daddy patted her knee. Neither of them looked at her.

Savannah stood and paced her parents' suite. "I'm so sorry. I didn't mean for this to spill out on Christmas day."

"How long have you known?" Daddy's voice sounded shaken.

"I've known for a number of weeks but decided not to say anything because you're my parents in every way that counts. And I love you."

"Then why bring it up now?"

"It just came out. I guess it was simmering below the surface and..." Savannah sank into her chair. "Will you tell me the story of my birth parents?"

Mother's head snapped up. "We'd rather not."

"Why?"

"Because you're our daughter, and that's all that matters."

"In the end, yes, I agree. You and Daddy are what matters, but I'd like to know."

"No. It is not necessary." The starch was back in Mother's spine.

Daddy leaned from his chair to squeeze Savannah's mother's hand. "She has a right to know, Anna."

Mother's blue eyes flashed him a disturbed look. "Fine, then, Henry, but don't look to me if this information backfires on us."

Daddy looked in Savannah's direction. Regret laced his eyes. "We should've told you sooner, but there's a reason we did not. Can you promise to keep this confidential?"

Savannah nodded.

"No one in our circle of friends knows that you're adopted because the truth could deeply affect your chance of a suitable marriage."

Savannah didn't care to marry anyone if she couldn't have Joseph, but Christmas day was not the time to declare that truth.

"Your mother and I tried and tried to have a family, but it was not to be." Raw emotions chased across his features as he blinked back tears. "And then one day, a set of circumstances brought you to our door..."

Savannah sat in rapt attention as the same story Emily had told unfolded. Only this time, it was a servant girl with no father in the picture whom Anna helped. The woman had died in childbirth, and Savannah's parents had deemed the precious girl a gift from heaven. They decided for the sake of the child's less-than-reputable background to fake a pregnancy. It was not hard to make Anna look pregnant, as the first five months of pregnancy was often concealed. Then the baby came early, and that bridged the gap further. By the time they started socializing again, Savannah was four months old and left with the nanny. No one ever questioned anything.

Savannah waited for her father to reveal that Emily was her auntie, but he did not. She would talk to Emily privately and give her parents the dignity of not demanding the identity of the man who had seduced Emily's sister. That man was not a father, and the scandal surrounding Savannah's birth would give her parents a fair amount of angst.

"So I'm of common birth?"

"You're our daughter." Daddy's words came out strong and firm.

"I understand that. And I thank you from my heart for all you've done for me. But maybe now when I tell you what I'm going to do, you'll understand."

A dark shadow fell across Daddy's eyes. "What is it?"

"Daddy, you know how I've been grappling for months now to find purpose and meaning in my life. I grumbled and complained that if only I was a man, I could join you and make some sense out of my existence."

He nodded.

Savannah turned and looked directly at her mother. "And Mother, you know how I've struggled to fit into your world of endless social gatherings, trips to Paris, and such."

"Why, I never..." Mother shook her head. "We give you all the opportunity life can offer and you—"

"I know. I seem ungrateful...but I'm not. It's just that something has been missing, and I now understand."

"Whatever do you mean?"

"Since I found Jesus in a way that is deeply personal, I long to join the ranks of those who work alongside the common person, the hurting soul, the disadvantaged one, but I can't even take care of myself."

"See, Henry?" She sent him a pointed look. "I told you taking religion too seriously is not good."

"Mother, this is my choice. And I want to start by learning how to take care of myself. To cook, clean, light a fire, wash my own clothes—"

Her mother jumped to her feet, shot across the room, and loomed over Savannah. "Have you gone mad? You would leave this life for that of a servant?"

Savannah stood and looked into her mother's eyes. "I'm willing. No common person will ever relate to me unless I understand the simple life."

"Why don't you choose to relate to those within your circle?" Father's voice boomed across the room. "If you love Jesus so much, stay where you are and be that light Reverend Bennett talked about this past Sunday, to your own kind."

Savannah shot him a startled glance. Daddy remembered so much of the service?

"Do the wealthy and privileged need God any less? We'll even give you money to start any charity you wish." Hope filled his eyes as he slid to the edge of his chair.

Savannah bowed her head and stared at the plush throw rug beneath her feet. She couldn't admit the whole of it—that she loved Joseph and hoped to learn how to be the kind of wife he needed so she could join him in his work. One kiss did not make a marriage proposal. Yet without revealing her feelings, her plan to learn the life of a servant wouldn't make sense.

"I'm in love with Joseph."

"You're what?" Her mother's voice reached screech level.

"He hasn't declared his love for me because he knows that our lives are so vastly different. But I'm sure he feels the same."

"Well, thank God for that small mercy." Daddy stood and pulled his hand through his hair.

"This whole thing is motivated by an infatuation?" Mother paced back and forth. "Henry, talk some sense into her."

Savannah straightened her spine. "This is not an infatuation. I do love him. And with or without a future with him, I want to learn how to take care of myself. That part I'm doing for me, but if it leads to more with Joseph, then so be it."

"And just how do you propose to obtain the experience of a servant?" Mother asked.

"I'd like to take turns at home in each area...the kitchen, housekeeping, laundry—"

"Stop right there." Mother held up her hand. "We'd be the laughingstock of New York society if this ever leaked out. And servants talk." She turned to Daddy, who stood there with a grim look on his face. "Henry? Do something."

He shook his head. "Today is not the day for this. We're due over at Moss Cottage shortly." He pulled his watch from his vest pocket. "We wouldn't want to offend the Struthers by being late, and then we have Christmas dinner at seven in the dining room."

"You're right, Henry, this is supposed to be a cheerful day, and it has become far from it." Mother glared at Savannah. "If you'll excuse us, we must prepare ourselves."

Savannah longed to hug them both and tell them how much she loved them, but she had been dismissed. "I'll be waiting in my room."

"You're going in that?"

Savannah turned back. "This is one of my best gowns. I had Emily prepare it in advance."

"But what about all the new ones you just received? Surely, you could pick one of those, so we don't look like paupers with you wearing the same dress as you did to the Gould's afternoon tea."

A heavy sigh escaped Savannah's lips. This changing so many times a day was exhausting, but she had no intention of fighting with Mother any further. She walked over and picked up one of the dresses and coordinating hats. "This is very lovely. Please send

Emily my way when you're done. I may need a little help."

The click of the door behind her brought instant tears. She had not meant to get into all of this on Christmas day. They must think her a perfectly horrid daughter.

CHAPTER 17

The clubhouse dining room was decorated beautifully with wreaths, garlands, pine boughs on the fireplace mantel, and glowing candles. Divine smells of roasted turkey, seafood, and both savory and sweet dishes wafted in from the kitchen. Savannah surveyed the room and found Joseph, who sat with different guests rather than at an assigned table. Seemed he was much more popular when he was not preaching.

When her gaze landed on him, a ripple of delight ran from tip to toe. Her breath cut off and chest tightened as his eyes found hers across the room. Mr. Pulitzer, sitting beside him, followed his gaze and said something. Joseph looked back at him, and they both laughed. Joseph didn't look her way again.

How would she get him alone if he kept avoiding her? Savannah slid into her chair beside Father, and he gave her a quick hug. She leaned into his shoulder. "I love you."

"And I you."

There was so much warmth in his smile that a sting prickled behind her eyes. She had no desire to disappoint either of her parents, but it seemed inevitable.

The meal started with terrapin soup, fresh oysters, and a grapefruit salad. Then rounds of turkey, quail, stuffing, and filet of beef was served with mashed potatoes and a medley of vegetables. By the time dessert was offered with a choice of fruit salad, ice cream, or assorted pies and pastries, Savannah's corset stays cut into her flesh. She shook her head while Aunt Mary piled each option onto her own plate.

Savannah's back was to Joseph, but she faced the entryway of the dining room. She kept her eyes discreetly trained in that direction. Joseph would not escape her this evening. His present was safely tucked in her reticule. She had only one Christmas wish, and that was to give the gift to him.

Mother and Father rose from the table, but thankfully, Aunt Mary was still finishing her desserts.

"We're going to retire to the parlor for a bit and then head to bed. I have a golf game first thing tomorrow morning." Father patted her shoulder before leaving, but Mother walked by with her head held high, still obviously upset with Savannah.

Please, God, help my parents understand. And give me a few moments alone with Joseph to share my heart. I will bend to Your will Lord no matter how difficult, but please make it clear.

"Savannah, are you listening to me?" Aunt Mary's voice hitched up an octave.

"Sorry, Auntie. My mind is a little scattered these days."

"Could it be that handsome young preacher walking this way who has your concentration?"

"He's headed this way?" Savannah refused to turn around and stare.

"He was, but Hattie interrupted him. Oh, now he's changed direction."

Aunt Mary called out, "Reverend Bennett. Over here." She beckoned him with one hand and pushed the rest of her dessert in front of Savannah with the other. "Let me handle this," she whispered.

Savannah chanced a glance. Joseph looked like he'd been summoned to the gallows, but he made his way over.

"Would you be so kind as to sit with my niece until she's finished her dessert? I'm exhausted and don't want to leave her at the table alone." Aunt Mary stood up, giving Savannah a sly wink, and bustled off before Joseph could decline.

It took everything Savannah had not to burst out in laughter. For her aunt to give up even a bite of dessert was a huge sacrifice. Savannah picked up the fork and played along.

Joseph sank into the chair beside her.

Just like that, God had answered her prayer, but now she was tongue-tied. She forced a bite of pie down her throat. "Have you been avoiding me, Joseph Bennett?"

"Nothing like getting right to the point." He smiled but it did not reach his eyes. "Yes. I have been keeping my distance."

Savannah's cheeks flushed hot, and tears pricked behind her eyelids. She could not speak.

"This whole friendship was a mistake for a number of reasons, and we both know it." His tone was abrupt and cold.

Savannah had to get out of there before she burst into tears. She stood abruptly. "I understand."

Her rush from the dining room, through the lobby, and across the veranda would not be deemed ladylike, but she didn't care. Shrouded in the bushes of the gardens, she allowed her tears free rein. Deep, guttural sobs welled from her soul. Joseph would never be hers.

"Please don't cry."

Savannah turned.

Joseph stood before her. A thin wash of light from the clubhouse and the clear moonlit sky brushed softly over his features. "I never meant to hurt you. But avoiding you is the only way I can ensure..." He stepped forward and drew her into his embrace. He cradled her face in his large hands and thumbed the tears away.

Savannah's breath shallowed out as he leaned in closer.

"That I don't do this..." His lips dropped to hers. His

kiss was like a touch of flame to fuel. Explosive. He crushed her closer. There was no mistaking the message. Warm. Needy. Passionate.

She had only one response—to meet him kiss for pleasurable kiss. Her arms circled the muscled column of his neck. His embrace made her soar and melt. Love swept through her being with an intensity that terrified her. He had burrowed his way into her heart, her head, that deepest part of her soul, and she didn't know how she would live without him.

A guttural groan came from deep within his chest as he pulled free. "And now you know."

She pulled him close, unable to resist one more time. His powerful arms wrapped around her, sheltering her from the cruelty of their very different worlds. Her hands mapped his face—the hard chisel of his chin with the stubble of a day's growth of beard—before running through his hair. She breathed in his wonderful woodsy scent. "I love you, Joseph Bennett."

His eyes darkened. The air between them tingled with tension-filled sparks. "And I love you, Savannah Ensworth, but—"

"No *but*s today."

She brushed his lips with aching tenderness. They kissed long and lingering, savoring each other. With tearing slowness, his mouth left hers.

"I have something for you." Savannah dug inside her reticule and pulled out the wrapped box. She handed it to him, but he stood holding it without moving. "Open it," she encouraged.

He unwrapped the bow and lifted the lid. The pocket watch gleamed in the moonlight. He pulled it out and fingered the embossed gold before opening it. "I know quality when I see it. And I bet this would take a year of my wages." He closed it and slipped it back in the box.

"Do you like it? I wanted to give you something special to remind you of the day you first kissed me." Her words rushed out. "So that when we're old and gray, our grandbabies will hear of *you, me and the Marshes of Glynn* and how God—"

"But this extravagant pocket watch is just another example of the differences between us...why I was not wrong in keeping my distance."

"What are you saying?"

"I'm saying what I've said from the first day I laid my eyes on you and instantly knew an impossible love."

"I know you could find a more suitable helper, but I could learn how to cook, to clean, to do what everyday people do."

"No. You're right where God has placed you."

"But—"

He pressed a finger over her lips. "You said no *but*s. And yet you, my dear Savannah, are the ocean...and I am but a wave." He kissed her forehead. "You are the rose, and I am but the cumbersome thorn in your life." He dropped a kiss on her protesting lips. "And you are the air, and I am but a breath." He kissed each cheek, then pressed the gift back into her hand. "I can't take this. Just like you—it was never meant for someone as common as me."

He turned and walked into the black of night.

CHAPTER 18

*J*oseph paced back and forth in his small bedroom on the fourth floor of the clubhouse. He had to get off this island. Savannah was too much of a temptation. Didn't the Good Book instruct to flee temptation? If he stayed another week as planned for their New Year's gala, he would lose the battle. With even a moment in her intoxicating presence, he could hear himself now, proposing marriage and giving in to her lofty ideas of a love that could never be.

A deep agony obsessed his heart and preoccupied his mind. How could he possibly do the Lord's work in this state? He had to let her go, and the sooner the better.

He knew just what he needed to do—join that golf game Mr. Joseph Pulitzer had suggested, where he would come face to face with Savannah's father. If he was honest with the man, maybe he'd help him get out of his obligation to preach one more Sunday.

He changed quickly, headed down the steps at breakneck speed, and hurried to the nine-hole golf course. Due to his inexperience, Joseph's short game was abysmal, but with his athletic ability, he could hold his own in the long game. His main goal was a moment alone with Savannah's father. He prayed that no one else had taken that fourth spot.

"Ah, you made it, after all," Joseph Pulitzer said. "Now there will be a Joseph Senior and Joseph Junior."

"You will always be Mr. Pulitzer to me." Joseph shook his hand, then extended his hand in turn to Mr. Baker and to Mr. Ensworth.

As he returned the gesture, Savannah's father looked straight into his eyes, as though he was assessing the enemy.

"Shall we?" Mr. Pulitzer stroked his full beard as they moved to the first tee. He lifted his round-rimmed spectacles that hung from a chain in his pocket and pressed them tightly against the bridge of his nose. "Let's get this game done early, before the activity on this island ramps up and too many noises distract from my game." He made light of how sensitive he was to sound, but Joseph knew from a deep discussion with him how debilitating the problem was.

Being the first to tee off, Mr. Baker walked with a slight limp up to the tee box. His distinguished horseshoe moustache met his long sideburns, with his chin smartly shaved. His first ball soared straight as a pin down the middle of the fairway.

Joseph hung back. He wanted to tee off last. He cared little about the game but everything about a moment with Mr. Ensworth. He prayed for a shot or two that would bring their balls close in proximity.

God answered that prayer on the fourth hole, as they awaited both Mr. Pulitzer's and Mr. Baker's shots up onto the green.

Joseph sidled close to Savannah's father. "I have to be honest with you, Mr. Ensworth. I came golfing today for only one reason...to talk to you."

The man's bushy brows bunched together. "I'm not sure I share the sentiment. Seems you have besotted my daughter when a bigger mismatch could not be found."

"I never meant to. I had no idea a man could fall so hard in so short a time."

"So you love her?"

"I do."

"Then I'm wondering if your love is strong enough to do right by her." His voice was curt and unyielding.

"I understand what you're asking. I love your daughter with all my heart." He dug his hand through his thick hair. "However, I'm wise enough to know it can never be. If you could talk to the powers that be, get me out of my commitment to preach next Sunday, and arrange a way off this island, I'd be most grateful."

"You'd willingly leave ahead of schedule?"

"I *need* to leave ahead of schedule. I don't want to

hurt your daughter any more than I already have." The thought of her tears in the moonlight the night before shot a pang of sorrow ripping through his heart. What he was about to do would be even worse.

"You're an honorable man." Mr. Ensworth took his shot, and the ball stopped just short of the pin.

Was he? If he had never allowed that first kiss...then he would not have the endless hunger, the craving for more, the insatiable need. He hit the ball, and it soared to the other side of the green and rolled down the far bank to the fairway beyond.

Mr. Ensworth smiled. "You need to work on your short game, young man."

They walked toward the green. It was not the golf game Joseph needed to work on, but the strength to say goodbye. "What I need most is to get away from the one woman who could convince a poor reverend that somehow, he could fit into this life. And we both know that's not possible."

"I will make it happen, and I know just the man to fill in on Sunday." He clapped his shoulder. "I appreciate that you love my daughter enough to do what is best for her."

"I do." As the words slipped out of his mouth, a mad sorrow gripped his heart. He would never see Savannah again. He could not risk it.

*J*oseph was gone. Savannah couldn't believe what Elizabeth and Walter had told her. He had not even said goodbye, but a wrapped gift and a letter sat on the side table next to her bed. The tears hadn't stopped long enough for her to see through the blur. Hours passed with her face down on the bed. Sobs wrenched from her body. How could he give up on them like that?

Her mother, then her father, then Emily, and now Elizabeth banged on her locked door.

"Come on, Savannah. Let me in," Elizabeth pleaded.

"Go away."

"I will not. I insist you let your best friend in. And I will sit on a chair outside this room until you unlock this door."

Fine. Savannah did not move.

Every hour on the hour, Elizabeth knocked on the door. "I'm still here. If you don't eat, I don't eat. But it's almost dinner and I'm hungry."

"Please, Elizabeth. Give me this time alone."

"Have you opened the letter and gift?"

"No."

"But Savannah, he said it would explain everything."

"There's no excuse for him leaving without talking to me." Anger tightened Savannah's voice. "He obviously doesn't feel the same about me as I do for him."

"I think he does."

Savannah marched to the door and swung it open. "My best friend is going to side with Joseph rather than with me?"

Elizabeth walked in. "I'm not siding with him, but I do understand his dilemma." She walked around the bed to where the letter sat on top of the gift and opened the envelope. She pulled out the letter and held it out. "Read it."

Savannah wiped the heel of her palm across her tear-drenched face. "I don't want to—"

"Yes, you do. I'm going down to the dining room kitchen to get us each a plate of food, and when I come back, you had better have read this and be ready to eat."

Savannah snatched the letter. "Some friend you are."

"I can be as stubborn as you if the situation warrants it." Elizabeth stood with her hands on her hips. "He agonized over the words...that much I know. At least be brave enough to read them." She moved across the room and quietly shut the door behind her.

Savannah sank onto the edge of the bed. Her gaze dropped to the paper in her trembling hand.

Dearest Savannah,

I'm so sorry that I'm not talking to you in person, but there is a limit to my strength where you're concerned. When I'm in your presence, I can't think straight, nor would I have the courage to do what I know is best for you.

In a wonderful month, I fell deeply in love with you. To be honest, it happened the moment I laid eyes on you sitting in that pew so regal and captivating. Then I met you and had the privilege of getting to know the person, the brilliant mind, behind the beautiful face, and the attraction became like a river's springtime madness pulling me along in its powerful current.

I always wondered why I couldn't feel what other women seemingly felt for me. Now I know it's as my dad said. "We Bennett men don't fall easily, but when we do, we fall in complete abandon."

I shall never love again.

Tears blurred Savannah's vision and splashed upon the fragile paper. She wiped the wetness away, but it blotched the ink. He did love her as much as she loved him.

But...

Oh, how she hated that word. It brought nothing but sorrow.

I know how you hate the word but.

She smiled through the tears. He was once again reading her mind.

Our two worlds collided for a moment...a rare, beautiful, perfect moment in time that will forever impact my heart, but sadly, was never meant to redirect the trajectory of our destiny.

God placed you in a unique family and circle of influence. I have been placed in a far different world. Both of us will go on to do the Lord's work where He has planted us. You are a beautiful woman of God whom I know will do great things for His kingdom.

I pray you will find a man who will be worthy of your vivacious, loving, free spirit, and together you will find much joy and create a beautiful family of your own.

I pray this small Christmas gift will ever lead you onward until that great someday when we shall meet again on the other side. Where there will be no societal rules, nor manmade walls, and we shall forever be friends among the many who love and worship our dear Jesus Christ.

With much love,
Always,
Joseph

Curiosity got the better of her, and she unwrapped the heavy gift. As she lifted the lid of the box, she found nestled in a piece of soft cloth Joseph's prized Bible, the one in which he had underlined special verses and written all his notes along the sides, top and bottom. She had asked him about it once, and he had shared that he'd received the Bible when he was twelve and all through seminary had jotted down things he learned. There was no gift that could have meant more.

Savannah dropped her head in prayer and pulled the Bible close to her chest. She fully understood the sacrifice of this gift.

CHAPTER 19

Savannah looked around her parents' suite, her gaze anywhere but on them. "I want to go home, and I'm pleading with you to permit this one small request."

She had prayed long and hard the whole lonely month of January, and the idea had not abated. Even without Joseph in her life, she longed to follow through on her plan to learn how to take care of herself rather than bask in luxury.

"I don't like it." Mother shook her head. "You're not some common servant."

Savannah dared not remind her mother that she could have been a servant but for a twist in destiny orchestrated by the hand of God. She had pressed Emily and learned that she was indeed her niece. Their relationship had blossomed from that freeing moment of truth.

"With you both here on the island until April, the work back home will be at a minimum...a perfect time for me to learn."

"Why are you so stubborn? That preacher is long gone, and there's no need to try and fit in with his life." Mother's frown deepened.

"This is not about Joseph. This is about me learning to understand the different walks of life. What will it hurt for me to be more aware and, hopefully, more compassionate?"

"It is not done."

"But who makes these rules?"

"All right, you two, enough." Daddy's stern voice cut in and gentled as he turned to his wife. "Anna, our daughter has been so sad, and whether we admit it or not, she has suffered a heartache. Maybe a bit of hands-on work will be therapeutic in nature. I know when I get busy, it helps me."

Mother looked between them. She threw up her hands. "How can I fight you both? Fine, then, Savannah, go about cooking, cleaning, and gardening, and God knows whatever else suits your fancy, but don't come crying to me when your hands are ruined and your skin loses that porcelain sheen." She stomped to the door of the suite. "And Henry, when you escort her home, be sure the staff understand if they breathe a word of this, they will lose their position instantly." She slammed the door behind her.

Savannah turned to her father, who smiled before

he spoke. "Good thing your mother will have some time to cool down before I return to the island. Get packing. I will arrange the trip to Brunswick with Captain Clark for first thing tomorrow."

"Thank you, Daddy." Savannah gave him a big hug. She pulled out of his arms and made her way to the door.

"And Savannah?"

"Yes." Savannah turned back toward him.

"Do you promise that this has nothing to do with Joseph?"

Savannah thought long and hard before answering. She stared down at the plush lavender carpet. She wanted to assure him but could not. For deep within, hope still lived. "I don't know what the future holds, Daddy. Joseph seems to think I could never fit into his life, and as long as he believes that, there won't be a chance. But at the very least, I can be ready for whatever God has planned."

"Hmm, I thought as much."

"Are you going to tell Mother?"

"Let's just say...your mother is no fool. She protested so vehemently because she fears losing you. And so do I."

"But does it have to mean you lose me if I chose a different lifestyle?"

He shook his head and rubbed his chin. "I don't know how others would treat us. I've heard of many trying to buy their way into our circle but can't say I've heard of anyone leaving this lifestyle."

"Well, if others are snobbish enough to disown you for choices I make, are they really friends?"

"A lifetime of breeding, wealth, and thinking one is somehow elevated beyond the common person is a mindset not easily broken. Muddying those waters does not make us feel comfortable."

Savannah's heart wrenched. "Do you hear yourself, Daddy?"

"I do. And I've done some real soul-searching lately. The one thing that young man has proven is that he truly cares for you. He would never have left if he was drawn to the things you worry most men are interested in when they court you—the money, the lifestyle, the power. I have to admit, he impressed me. He truly wants what is best for you, and that means a lot to this father's heart."

Savannah's insides jumped. Perhaps her father's opinion could be swayed, but what of Joseph's? She had read and reread his letter so many times she had it memorized. He thought he was doing what was best for her by letting go, but he could not be more wrong. "As for Joseph's decision, there's little doubt, he could find a more suitable choice for a preacher's wife than me, and his resistance may be tied to that. Although I have hope, I'm not blind to the complications. And I do truly want to learn how to take care of myself regardless of how this goes."

"Then you shall, my darling." Daddy kissed her on the forehead. "Just don't throw the baby out with the bath water."

"Meaning?"

"We need you as much as you need us."

Savannah smiled. "So true. I shall always need both you and Mother." She gave her father another hug.

"But don't think your mother will be so easily persuaded."

"Oh, I know she won't, but she has you."

He laughed. "And you think I can sway that strong woman's mind?"

"She loves us both dearly, so there is hope."

"Yes, there is."

Savannah slipped from the room and made her way into her bedroom to prepare for her departure. She might not be happy, but she was filled with a peace she did not understand. God was working all things out for His glory. Her daddy's help was just one of those details. And if God wanted Joseph and her together, there was not a thing in the world that would stop their relationship.

She would learn what she needed to be the perfect reverend's wife. If Joseph still rejected her, then so be it. At least she'd have given it her all. Because if he thought she could love another any easier than he could, he was badly mistaken.

∼

A sense of satisfaction came over Savannah. Her hands were gloriously ruined. She turned them one way and then the other. All the expensive creams in the world would not change what scrubbing, cleaning, gardening, and cooking had done, but over these past three months, she had never been more content or exhausted at the end of each day.

The servants had responded with reluctance at first, but after she met their every challenge and every job with exuberance, that hesitancy had faded. She'd won them over. These people were no longer nameless faces moving in and out of rooms. She knew all about their children, their spouses, their struggles and hopes. They were her friends.

Mother and Father would be home from Jekyll Island any day now, but she had something she needed to do before they returned and tried to talk her out of it.

CHAPTER 20

𝒥oseph moved about the small parsonage, tidying his dishes from breakfast and the night before. A sense of abject loneliness filled his heart. The one woman he had finally fallen in love with would never be his.

He had prayed and fasted and poured himself into his work. Each parishioner had received a home visit. His sermons were spot on. His preaching had never been more Spirit led, filled with truth and challenge, sprinkled with compassion and love. And yet...he was not at peace.

The way he had run from Savannah no longer felt right. He had judged her based only on her upbringing, not on the woman whom God was shaping and molding. The Holy Spirit was revealing Joseph's own brand of prejudice, and he was grieved.

If God saw all humanity the same, and Joseph

fought for the rights of the poor to have the same opportunities as the wealthy, then how was it any different for the rich to have the same opportunity to live the simple life if they chose? He had never given Savannah the right to choose.

But how to right the wrong? He didn't know where she lived in New York City and would most likely have the door slammed in his face even if he sleuthed the information.

Savannah and her parents would most likely still be on Jekyll Island, but the warm days of spring would soon be calling them home. The past four months had given him time to work out his necessary apology. Still, if he saw her again, he might throw all common sense to the wind and beg her to leave her life of luxury and love a poor preacher. His feelings for her had not abated, only grown stronger.

What was God doing? No matter how much he prayed for the desire to leave him, the only thing he got from God was how much he owed Savannah an apology. But did he have the courage to be in her presence with all the emotion that swirled in his heart?

The sunshine beckoned him outdoors. He would sit in the warmth and work on his sermon notes. He grabbed his new Bible, with the reminder of how much he missed his old one. Was Savannah learning and growing in the Lord? He prayed so.

He settled himself on his favorite chair, situated on a small brick courtyard surrounded by lawn. The protective arms of a sprawling oak shaded the gathering strength of the sun. He laid his Bible on the small table beside him and started as he always did...in prayer. When he opened his eyes, he had to blink twice. His heart immediately kicked like a stallion against the walls of his chest.

There stood the love of his life, Savannah, with a picnic basket hanging off one arm, clothed in the nondescript dress of a common servant and a smile as wide as the Atlantic Ocean. He soaked in the sight, unable to move, to speak, to even think. He was afraid to blink for fear she'd disappear. Never had she looked more beautiful.

~

Savannah had shared her heart and her story with her new friends. The household groomsman who knew New York City inside and out was only too pleased to aid in finding the small parish church Joseph oversaw. The cook cheered her on as she put together the perfect picnic basket. And her quest for the day had the encouragement of each servant in the Ensworth household. Now that she stood before Joseph, all she had to do was find the courage and the words.

Joseph jumped up. "Savannah, is that really you?"

A tremor tripped up her spine at the rich, low timbre of his voice. Oh, how she had missed that. Her heart thumped in her chest, and the tug of it reached for him. She twirled in her servant's dress. "Do you like? It's what I've been wearing the past three months."

His brows bunched, but the admiration in his eyes could not be missed. "Last three months?"

"I've been back home since the end of January and had the most rewarding time of my life. But before all that, would you agree to my company over a picnic lunch I've brought to share?"

"I'd be honored. I didn't know if you'd talk to me after the way I left. I've wanted to apologize for months now. I'm truly sorry."

Savannah nodded and kept things cool when she could've jumped for joy. He was regretting his hasty departure. That was positive. "It was rather sudden and most ungentlemanly of you. But I have grown to understand the wherefore and why and, hopefully, rectified the biggest problem." Strength was building within her.

He cleared his throat. "The biggest problem?"

She wasn't ready to answer that yet, so she pulled a checkered cloth from the top of her basket. "Would you be so kind as to spread this?" She handed him the blanket. "Underneath this beautiful oak is a perfect spot."

As soon as he was done, she dropped down and patted the area beside her. He stood without moving.

"Come, Joseph. I won't bite, and I do have a wonderful lunch. I cooked the whole thing."

His eyes popped open wide, and she almost burst out laughing as he cautiously sat beside her.

"Let's see...I have fried chicken, beef meat pie, homemade bread, dressed eggs, and strawberry preserves with chocolate cake for dessert. Oh, and a jug of lemonade—all made by little old me." She flashed him what she hoped would be a saucy grin.

"You made everything...even this?" He held up the jar of strawberry preserves.

"Yes. But I admit I had to order the strawberries from Florida to accomplish that feat."

Anticipation gnawed at her insides, but Savannah managed to make small talk through the meal, sprinkling in the knowledge she had gained over the past three months. "I feel confident I can now run a small household of my own all within a budget. You just wouldn't get strawberries in March. You'd have to wait until they're in season." She laughed to cover up the anxiety that was screaming through her veins. What if he rejected her again?

"This meal is amazing. And I see you've learned all you set your mind to." His gaze swept over her with such longing it made her mouth go dry. He jumped to his feet and paced back and forth. "But why?"

Savannah stood and walked straight up to him, their bodies almost touching. He stopped all movement. "Why do you think, Joseph? Are you that blind that you can't see I'd move heaven and earth to be with you? I know you could find a more suitable preacher's wife, but I'm in the Word daily, and I've learned some hymns on the piano. I've found great joy in befriending people from all walks of life. But most importantly, I—"

Her words were cut off by the crush of his mouth to hers. She melted into his embrace, her senses running sharp. The fire of his touch, the woodsy scent of pine-soap-washed skin, the taste of his lips made her racing blood sing with pleasure. He traced kisses from her forehead down her cheek, to the pulse in her throat that fluttered like hummingbird wings before landing on her lips yet again. In between kisses, he whispered over and over, "I love you, Savannah. I love you."

As he pulled free, every part of her body objected with vigor. "I love you, Joseph Bennett. And I don't care what your letter said. My heart will not rest in the care of any other man."

"I now know why God has not granted me peace in letting you go. My heart has literally ached for you." He cupped her face gently in his hands and leaned his forehead to rest against hers. "I can't believe you're actually here."

"And best you remember that for the rest of your life. Because I'm not going anywhere."

He kissed her lips one more time before stepping back. "What about your parents?"

"Daddy already knows, and Mother has a very good idea why I was so bent on learning how to care for myself. And God is a God of miracles, is He not? Since He brought us together, my parents are His problem, not ours."

He pulled her into his arms and touched his lips softly to her hair. "I will never again limit the power of God."

"To be clear, I'm not sure how this will go with my parents, but I'm prepared to leave everything and cleave to you. Are you willing to do right by me?"

Joseph dropped to one knee and took her hand in his. "Savannah, these past few months have been the worst of my life. I found my soulmate and then lost her. I experienced a glimpse of something I never had before—the wonder, the potential, the strength a man and woman who love each other can experience together. I don't have much to offer other than extravagant love...but will you walk this life beside me as my partner, my equal, my wife?"

"Yes. Yes. And yes."

She pulled him to his feet and lifted her eyes to the heavens. "A wise man once quoted a line I shall never forget. A line that gave me courage when I burnt my first meal, and my clothes came out dirty after I washed them, and all the other failures I endured before I had success...

'I will fly in the greatness of God as the marsh hen flies,

In the freedom that fills all the space 'twixt the marsh and the skies.'

I figured if the marsh hen could trust God for meeting the simplest of needs and fly in freedom, so, too, could I."

Joseph's warm arms came solidly around her. "Did I

tell you, Savannah dearest, how extremely proud I am of you?"

She giggled. "No, but you may start now."

He dipped his head, and their lips met in a dance as old as time.

Did you enjoy this book? We hope so!
Would you take a quick minute to leave a review where you purchased the book?
It doesn't have to be long. Just a sentence or two telling what you liked about the story!

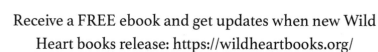

Receive a FREE ebook and get updates when new Wild Heart books release: https://wildheartbooks.org/newsletter

Don't miss the next book in the Romance at the Gilded Age Resorts Series!

A Summer on Bellevue Ave
By Lori Dudley

Chapter 1

NEW YORK, NEW YORK
JUNE 7, 1895

A scream and tumbling sound woke Wesley Astor Jansen. He jolted upright from his desk and swiped at the paper that stuck to his cheek.

Had he dreamed the noise? Who else was here?

He tilted his ear up and listened, but in the office of Jansen and Sons Oil and Energy Engineering, not even the janitorial staff stirred. The oil lamp on the corner of his desk burned low. He flicked open his gold pocket watch and held it near the sputtering light.

Quarter after three in the morning. He snapped the lid shut and tucked the timepiece back into his suit pocket.

His copy of the signed marriage agreement he'd struggled for the better part of an hour to read though lay scattered across his desk. He gathered the pages into a pile and turned to file them in his side drawer.

Odd. The drawer stood open. Had he left it that way?

He slid the papers into the first folder, then closed and locked the compartment. It was late. He should head home. Light sparkled off the remaining bubbles still bursting in his half-finished champagne glass. He brought the glass over to the sideboard for the staff to clear.

It had been a solitary victory celebration after obtaining Mr. Klein's blessing to marry his daughter—a hard-won feat. Mr. Klein's ruthless business and social dealings sought one-sided advantages, but Wesley, too, could be relentless. A financial investment closed the deal with Klein & Co. manufacturing their line of motor cars with Jansen and Sons' unique grade of gasoline. They both signed, and the only stipulation was for Wesley's money to be returned if Amanda declined his offer of marriage.

Paying for his bride didn't sit well with Wesley. If Amanda discovered what her father asked of him and the dollar amount, she'd be horrified. In the end, he'd have paid even more because he loved Amanda, and a Jansen-Klein business alliance would profit them both.

Grander festivities would take place tomorrow evening after he proposed and Amanda accepted.

Wesley yawned and ran his hand down his face. He'd been having some dream. Amanda had slipped away for a reprieve from gathered guests and stood on the balcony of his New York City mansion peering down at Central Park below. Her dark hair was pulled up and woven with tiny pearls. Her long, graceful neck

SNEAK PEEK: A SUMMER ON BELLEVUE AVE

beckoned to be nuzzled. The silk material of her gown ruffled in the night breeze, emphasizing her delicate curves.

He touched the small of her back. She turned, greeting him with that shy smile of hers that slowly widened, until she glowed like the full moon. Few people witnessed Amanda's true joy—tiny, polite grins, yes—but he was one of the few blessed to feel the full radiance of her smile and laughter.

He swooped in and stole a kiss, brushing her velvet lips with his, and a thrill ran through his midsection like a player crossing the goal line. He couldn't wait to give her his last name and wake each morning with her beside him, tussled and sleepy-eyed. He leaned in to deepen their kiss, craving her feminine softness. The railing broke, and she screamed. His arms swiped air, and she tumbled into darkness below.

The scream must have been part of his dream, but by Jove, it had sounded real.

A groan resounded outside his office, raising the fine hair on his neck.

Wesley jumped to his feet and grabbed the oil lamp. He darted from the room and peered over the banister of the office's second-story gallery down into the open foyer below. "Who's there?"

Retreating footsteps slapped the tile floor of the back hall, and a door slammed. Wesley had turned to give chase when a moan below stopped him.

Someone was hurt.

He leaned over the railing and extended the lamp out past his head. A form lay crumpled at the bottom of the curved stairs. Her skirts twisted around her body, and her leg bent at an odd angle.

Wesley dashed down the plush red carpet lining the marble stairs. He dropped to his knees next to the woman sprawled on her stomach on the cold tile.

"Are you all right?" Of course, she wasn't. He brushed her hair away from her face but didn't recognize her.

Her eyelashes fluttered, and a moan issued through her red lips.

Should he move her? Flip her over? "Where are you hurt?"

Her eyelids stopped moving.

He shook her, but she made no sound or movement. His hands quaked as he felt for her pulse, and he held his breath. A light throb against his fingertips said she was alive.

Thank God.

His heart banged against his ribcage, vibrating his entire being. He jumped to his feet. Who would he find at this hour to aid her? The quiet foyer and empty building mocked him. The doctor lived five streets over, but was it wise to leave her? He ran to the entrance and flung open the main doors, the same ones he'd locked after letting himself in.

He leaned out into the damp night air. A street

cleaner pushed his cart along Fifth Avenue, and a drunk couple clung to each other, stumbling into a back alley.

"You, there." He pointed to the street cleaner. "Twenty dollars awaits you if you fetch Doctor Collins on Fifty-Ninth and Sixth."

The street cleaner dropped his broom and ran.

"Twenty dollars, you say?" The other man pushed away from the woman and sprinted remarkably well in his drunken state toward Fifty-Ninth.

"Cad." The woman spat in the man's wake and stomped down the side street.

Wesley re-entered the lobby. He grabbed another lamp, and turning the wick up, knelt beside the woman.

She dressed formally as if she'd attended a performance at the Metropolitan Opera House, but seated in the pit, not the upscale balcony box seats. A plume of feathers protruded from a cockeyed hat, askew from her fall. Rouge stained her cheeks and lips.

Who was she? A customer who'd been locked inside? A robber or thief? Someone had run. Had that been her accomplice?

He shrugged off his jacket and folded it into a square. Gently lifting her head, he slid the makeshift pillow underneath so her face no longer lay on the cold marble tile. He scooted back to put a hand's length between them.

What kind of gossip would spread about such a

woman found sprawled on the floor of Jansen and Sons? Would it affect business? His reputation?

Wesley's stomach soured.

Would it affect Mr. Klein's blessing to marry Amanda?

Surely, once the woman woke, she'd explain to the authorities why she was here and what she'd been doing. He'd been asleep, but that weak alibi wouldn't be enough to squash any rumors.

The image of his open desk drawer flashed in his memory, and a troubling premonition slithered down his spine. If she'd fallen down the stairs, then she must have been on the same floor as him. Had she been in his office?

Wesley glanced over his shoulder. A slipper lay about halfway up the stairs. He retrieved it, laying it next to the woman. A reticule was hooked on her arm, and a paper stuck out of the top bearing the Jansen company letterhead symbol. He loosened the drawstring and peeked within.

Several papers had been folded and shoved inside. He removed them and flipped through the pages. A company balance sheet and income statement lay among some of the proprietary paperwork. He recognized double-underlined numbers, and the corresponding lines showed the company's total equity and net income. Behind those reports, he found what resembled stock purchases, though the words were difficult to make out, and the negotiated gentleman's agreement between Klein & Co. and Jansen and Sons that he'd signed tonight.

Was she a competitor's spy or sent by a labor union leader to rally support for a strike? These weren't merely from his files but from the office of his brother —the head of marketing and sales—also. He stared at the unconscious woman in a new light. She'd been trying to bamboozle them.

Where was the doctor?

He stomped to the front door and flung it wide. The doctor's coach barreled down the street, and the horses skidded to a stop in front of the building. The carriage door was flung open, and the doctor exited with black bag in hand, still buttoning his coat.

"Doctor Collins." Wesley raised his hand in greeting. "Right this way." He gestured to the lobby and stepped aside to let the man pass.

The doctor pushed up his spectacles and knelt beside the woman. "What happened here?" He lifted her wrist, felt for a pulse, and nodded.

Wesley shrugged. "I fell asleep at my desk, awoke to a scream, and found her like this."

"I see." He moved the lamp closer to her face and pulled her eyelids apart. He peered into each eye. "Was she conscious?"

"Not entirely. She moaned a few times." Wesley stepped back and leaned on the curved newel post at the bottom of the stairs.

"We'll need to get her to the hospital." He nodded to the door. "Tell my coachman to bring the stretcher."

Wesley jumped at the chance to feel useful and to leave the bizarre scene before him. The coachman and footman retrieved the stretcher, and Wesley held the door open for them to pass.

"Her tibia appears broken. We must flip her over, but I'll need to stabilize the leg. Mr. Jansen, please hold her head, and my coachman and footman will handle the heavy lifting."

Wesley crouched, and on the count of three, adjusted the woman's head as they guided her onto the stretcher.

The doctor sent a footman back to the carriage for a brace while he checked the woman over for any other sustained injuries.

An officer appeared in the open entrance and rapped on the door. "I saw the doctor's coach and the lamplight through the window. Is there a problem?" He crossed his arms and glared at Wesley as if he'd already been condemned without a trial.

A cold prickle raised the hairs on the back of his neck.

"Who's the lady?" The officer inclined his head toward the stretcher.

"I don't have the foggiest." Wesley recounted his story, including the papers found in her reticule, but as he envisioned the events through the eyes of the officer, the alarm sounding in Wesley's mind increased.

A nicely dressed woman lay on the floor, unconscious, her hair mussed and lipstick smudged, which likely had happened during the fall but had the look of being smeared during a midnight tryst. The officer asked where Wesley had been, and he showed his workspace where he'd fallen asleep on his desk. The officer's gaze lingered on the half-drunk champagne glass. He closed the office door as they exited. To prevent evidence tampering?

"You're considering this a crime scene?" Wesley hated the squeak in his voice.

What would happen when word spread? How would it affect Jansen and Sons' reputation and business dealings—especially the promotion of their new gasoline? What about Amanda? Her father? Their engagement to be announced? He placed his hand on the wall to not double over at the sick feeling in his stomach.

The officer's lips twisted into a sardonic smile. "Don't worry. Someone's father will pay to have this slid under the rug. Someone always does with you knickerbocker types."

"What about the documents in her purse?"

"Easily could have been planted." The officer held Wesley's gaze.

Wesley refused to squirm. "But they weren't."

Below, the men lifted the stretcher and carried the woman out of the lobby. The officer trotted down the stairs and exited the building. Wesley followed.

Morning sun crested the horizon, but overcast clouds turned the sky an eerie yellow-gray and hazed the glow of the oil lamps lining the street.

A spitting drizzle of late spring clung to Wesley's white linen tuxedo shirt, and cold seeped through without his jacket to warm him.

The woman on the stretcher stirred.

Wesley stepped closer, curious for a better look at the woman's alert face.

Her eyes opened, and she blinked as if trying to focus. "Why?" She snatched his shirtfront and twisted her grip.

"Who are you?" Wesley pulled back, but the woman held him with surprising strength.

"You said you loved me."

She mistook him for someone else. Maybe the man who ran out the back. "How did you get in the building?" He pried her fingers away. "Who accompanied you?"

Her eyes rolled back in her head, and her hand dropped.

He held the side of the stretcher, stalling the footmen carrying her. "What were you doing here?"

The officer pulled him away, and she was loaded into the bed of the carriage. The doctor climbed inside and closed the door.

The street sweeper lingered about, waiting for payment, and Wesley pulled out a twenty-dollar bill and passed it to him.

SNEAK PEEK: A SUMMER ON BELLEVUE AVE

A stranger who'd stood beside the doctor flipped a page of his notepad. "Mr. Jansen." He stepped forward. "Who was that woman, and how did she get injured?"

"I've never seen her before in my life." Bile rose in Wesley's throat.

"Why were you working so late at night?"

Wesley strode back into the building, unable to block the niggling that there was something familiar about the woman's face, nor the foreboding that his life had been ruined. He was used to talking his way out of debacles. As chief executive of operations, he'd finagled his way through negotiations, contracts, and lawsuits. He knew how to think fast and when to bluff or show his hand, but this fiasco landed a left hook from out of nowhere.

He peered up at the chandelier hanging from the gold-leafed circle pendant dripping with crystals and beseeched God. "Why now? Why, with so much hanging in the balance?"

Amanda.

The way the reporter's lips had curved, like a fox licking its lips, built pressure in Wesley's chest. He must explain the truth to Amanda before vicious gossip or the morning paper reached her. He grabbed his jacket off the floor, bolted up the stairs to his office, retrieving his hat, and rushed back down.

"Whoa, now. Where are you off to so fast?" The officer stood in the open foyer.

Wesley slowed his descent. "Sir?"

The loathing in the officer's gaze turned Wesley's stomach.

"The name's Detective Millis." He folded his arms. "And I have more questions for you."

AUTHOR'S NOTE

The history of Jekyll Island is fascinating, from the indigenous people to the arrival of Spanish explorers in 1510 who named the Island *Isla De Ballenas* (Whale Island), onward to the English occupation during the Colonial Era in 1733. The island was renamed during this time by General James Oglethorpe, who established the colony and wanted to honor his friend, Joseph Jekyll. However, the spelling remained incorrect for many years. Through the Plantation Era and into the Club Era during which this book takes place, the spelling of *Jekyl Island* contained only one *l*. It took the research of female members in 1929 to discover the spelling error. The state of Georgia promptly passed legislation to correct the spelling to *Jekyll*. Though the spelling during the period in which I am writing (1906-1907) would have been *Jekyl*, my publisher chose to use

AUTHOR'S NOTE

the current spelling, *Jekyll,* as there may be other books set on the island forthcoming.

The Jekyll Island Club came into existence on February 17, 1886. Fifty-three members purchased shares with a limit of a hundred members, with the goal to market the island as a winter retreat for the extremely wealthy. It was a raging success. The clubhouse was officially opened in January of 1888, and the island became an exclusive club to many of the world's wealthiest families. One could visit by invitation only. This "Millionaires' Hideaway" became the place some of the most powerful American financiers could relax in prestigious, undisturbed isolation. During its peak, the claim was made that its members controlled one-sixth of the world's wealth. This story takes place in the midst of the Club Era, which lasted from 1888 to 1942, before the island was sold back to the state of Georgia.

Though I have endeavored to stay historically accurate in this, and in the related series to come, this story is fictional. Savannah and her family are entirely birthed from the portals of my wild imagination, but some of the guests they visited, such as the Rockefellers, Maurices, Bakers, Goulds, Joseph Pulitzer, etc., are real people who were part of the Jekyll Island Club during the Club Era. For how could one write about a millionaires' club and not mention the actual millionaires?

Some of the employees, such as Club Superintendent Mr. Grob, Captain James Clark, or the ladies deco-

AUTHOR'S NOTE

rating the church, Aleathia and Ophelia, are real people who lived and worked there. The island, the clubhouse, the mansion-like cottages, and the flora and fauna have been meticulously researched to bring authenticity to this story. I hope I have done a good job of setting you in that place and time so you can feel, hear, smell, see, and be touched by the lives of the people who long ago walked upon that soil.

Today there is a causeway built through the beautiful Marshes of Glynn so visitors can access the island from the mainland by car. It is a popular tourist destination. I would highly recommend a trip to this Golden Isles barrier island. The historical district has been painstakingly restored and the clubhouse stands in all its original glory. From the variety of beaches to a photographer's heaven on Driftwood Beach, to the miles of bike trails, salt marshes, and abundant wildlife, this island is deemed one of the fifty most beautiful small towns in America. I could see why when I visited.

If you have not yet had the pleasure, I hope you will someday have the opportunity to step upon the soil where millionaires trod and bask in the same sunshine they did. Perhaps have high tea in the clubhouse or ride a bicycle on the hard-packed shores of the very beaches they enjoyed. For we are all God's beautiful creations. He sees not our money, our status, or our family connections...He sees our heart.

ABOUT THE AUTHOR

Blossom Turner is a freelance writer published in Chicken Soup and Kernels of Hope anthologies, former newspaper columnist on health and fitness, avid blogger, and novelist. She lives in a four-season playground in beautiful British Columbia, Canada, with gardening at the top of her enjoyment list. She has a passion for women's ministry, but having coffee and sharing God's hope with a hurting soul trumps all. She lives with her husband, David, of forty years. Blossom loves to hear from her readers. Visit her at blossomturner.com and subscribe to her monthly newsletter.

Don't miss Blossom's other book, a contemporary romance, *Anna's Secret*, a Word Guild semi-finalist.

Join Blossom's monthly newsletter where you can win prizes, receive a new recipe, or get a peek into her life: http://blossomturner.com

ACKNOWLEDGMENTS

To put in words my thank you to the amazing team at Wild Heart Books is next thing to impossible. To publisher Misty M. Beller and my wonderful editor, Denise Weimer, you have my sincerest thanks for elevating my work way beyond its original first draft. And thanks to unsung heroes like Sherri Johnson and Sarah Erredge, who work behind the scenes on marketing, memes, book covers, galley changes, etc. Wild Heart Books is a pleasure to write for. The company is well-run and the professionalism second-to-none.

To my critique partner, Laura Thomas, who spends hours combing through my story, thank you from my heart. And to my incredible support team who have become amazing friends, thank you for reading the ARC and then encouraging others to read by your wonderful reviews.

Thank you, dear readers. Without your faithful support and your readership, there would be no point in writing.

And as always, but by the grace of God go I. Without His outstretched hands of help each day when I sit down at the keyboard, I could not accomplish half of what I do. Thank you, Jesus, for being a living, breathing, wonderful part of my every day. Thank you for the gift of imagination. You are the best co-author any girl could ever have.

Support Team

If you enjoyed this book and love reading and would like to be a part of my Support Team as the next book launches, contact me through my web page at https://blossomturner.com under the "Contact" heading.

A Support Team member will receive a free advance copy of the next book *before* it is released and promises to support in the following ways...

- Read the book in advance and have it completed by release date.
- If you enjoy the book, leave a review on Bookbub and Goodreads before release date as soon as you are done reading. Right after the release date, copy that review onto the other retailers, Amazon, Kobo, Barnes and Noble, and Apple Books. I will send you all the links so that it is super easy.
- Promote ahead of time on social media, FB, Twitter, Instagram, or wherever. (I will send you memes to post before release date so

that everything will be simple. I will not inundate you with too many.)

I will have numerous prize draws for the support team members in which your name will be entered to win a free signed copy of the previous books in the series, a GC for Amazon. (Sorry, open to residents of Canada and the USA only.) I will try and make the process as fun as possible, and hopefully you will enjoy the read. Those of you who have joined my team before and left such wonderful reviews, I thank God for you and consider you a part of my writing family. I thank you in advance for joining me on this journey.

WANT MORE?

If you love historical romance, check out the other Wild Heart books!

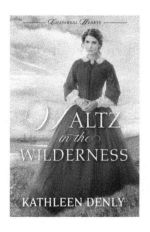

Waltz in the Wilderness by Kathleen Denly

She's desperate to find her missing father. His conscience demands he risk all to help.

Eliza Brooks is haunted by her role in her mother's death, so she'll do anything to find her missing pa—even if it means sneaking aboard a southbound ship. When those meant to protect her abandon and betray her instead, a family friend's unexpected assistance is a blessing she can't refuse.

Daniel Clarke came to California to make his fortune, and a stable job as a San Francisco carpenter has earned him more than most have scraped from the local goldfields. But it's been four years since he left Massachusetts and his fiancé is impatient for his return. Bound for home at last, Daniel Clarke finds his heart and plans challenged by a tenacious young woman with haunted eyes. Though every word he utters seems to offend her, he is determined to see her safely returned to her father. Even if that means risking his fragile engagement.

When disaster befalls them in the remote wilderness of the Southern California mountains, true feelings are revealed, and both must face heart-rending decisions. But how to decide when every choice before them leads to someone getting hurt?

A Matter of Trust by Winnie Griggs

When Lucy Ames rescues a stranger from being beaten and robbed, she can't just leave the man to die, but with her reputation in town already in tatters, how can she take this wounded man into her home? All she can do is what's right...and hope for the best. Unlike Lucy, her young charge, Toby, is delighted to have a man in the house. As much as Lucy wants the man gone, she can't begrudge him the father figure he never knew.

On a self-assigned mission to locate his nephew, Reed Wilder can't believe his luck when he realizes his beautiful rescuer is the strumpet who beguiled his arrow-straight brother. But she's not at all what he expected. She's independent and feisty and...captivating. Before either of them realize it, Lucy and Reed fall in love. But how can their relationship survive the secrets that plague them both?

∽

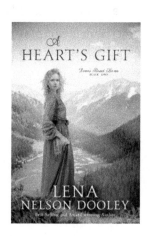

A Heart's Gift by Lena Nelson Dooley

Is a marriage of convenience the answer?

Franklin Vine has worked hard to build the ranch he inherited into one of the most successful in the majestic Colorado mountains. If only he had an heir to one day inherit the legacy he's building. But he was burned once in the worst way, and he doesn't plan to open his heart to another woman. Even if that means he'll eventually have to divide up his spread among the most loyal of his hired hands.

When Lorinda Sullivan is finally out from under the control of men who made all the decisions in her life, she promises herself she'll never allow a man to make choices for her again. But without a home in the midst of a hard Rocky Mountain winter, she has to do something to provide for her infant son.

A marriage of convenience seems like the perfect arrangement, yet the stakes quickly become much higher than either of them ever planned. When hearts become entangled, the increasing danger may change their lives forever.

Printed in the USA
CPSIA information can be obtained
at www.ICGtesting.com
LVHW011056270923
759395LV00008B/165